FADING COLOURS DEEP

MARK ALBRO

FADING
COLOURS DEEP

A Novel

Les éditions Europe

To Brian, my rock.
Always there

There is a magic made by melody:
A spell of rest and quiet breath, and cool
Heart, that sinks through fading colours deep
To the subaqueous stillness of the sea,
And floats forever in a moon-green pool,
Held in the arms of rhythm and of sleep.

"Because I hate that place. It makes me feel like a Silesian peasant harvesting turnips."

Horns honked; sirens wailed. Byron looked down on New Jersey bound traffic as it inched toward the Lincoln Tunnel.

His fiancée and soon-to-be brother-in-law conversed telephonically. The conversation burned his back. His fiancée's phone had a death ray.

"Yes, it's a real place, it was Prussian and now Polish."

All Charlotte and Percy's conversations left him stressed.

"Whatever. I'm not going there. If you want to shop with body odor organic people, be my guest. Goodbye."

People thought Byron's family magical. Even their eccentricities enchanted observers, and he had long been an outstanding eccentricity. Apt then, that he prepared to marry into a weird family. Byron's family always had that shiny old-money something that no one – especially people like the *nouveaux riches* Charlottes of this world – can imitate. His Great-Great Grandfather built their Upper East Side town-house, the décor of which resembled Charlotte's family condo in a tower in the way a classic Land Rover resembles a pimped-out Escalade. To the greater world Byron conveyed Episco-palian civility at a time when civility seemed in short supply. More than a few charities depended on his family.

"Are you taking in the view or ignoring me?" Charlotte asked.

"Both." He said, treading carefully, as one did with Char-lotte. He heard the click of her phone. "Are you taking a photo of me or the view?"

"Neither." She pointed toward her Siamese cat Mr. Darcy, who had curled on the bottom ledge of this panoramic 59th floor view of the Empire State Building and midtown Manhat-tan. "So," she sighed, "where do I put Claudia and her husband? It's crazy making."

He looked at his beautiful fiancée as she twirled a skein of her hair and doodled on the edge of a seating chart. Sitting beside her on an uncomfortable minimalist sofa, he inspected the chart for the wedding rehearsal dinner.

"I'm thinking there." She jabbed her pencil at two spots in a far corner.

"They'll know you're trying to hide them."

She gave him one of her looks. "There are two hundred and twenty people and two hundred and ten chairs."

"Where are we?"

"Here," she jabbed, "at the top, next to your grandmother and Aunt Olivia." Byron's paternal grandmother, who lived in rural Connecticut, kept her beauty as a *dame d'un certain âge* and rode broomsticks at night. To her face they called her Grandmother and behind her back, a variety of other things, the politest of which was Cow. Lovely Aunt Olivia, his father's sister, Byron liked. "Do we have to sit there? I *always* get stuck with Grandmother."

"You're the old woman whisperer. And think of it this way, if you're sitting at the same table, she can't talk behind your back."

"Where are mom and dad?"

"Here," she said, with a quick jab at the next table over, "with Ethan and Lauren, Duncan and Louise and Lauren's parents. Which is why your grandmother can't sit there."

"*Huh?*"

"Her mother's black."

"I know. We've been out to dinner with them."

"Your grandmother can't be trusted. God, I'll put a sleeping pill in her champagne if I can. She'll say something sneakily insinuating about how – what's Lauren's mother's name?"

"Isn't it on your chart?"

"No. It just says L's M."

"Cynthia."

"Right. She'll say something about Cynthia having an Italian surname, so she must have taken her husband's name or rattle on about those friends of hers who emigrated from South Africa."

"Like what? Cynthia was supposed to have an African surname at birth?"

"That's my point. She'll make her little racialisms because she can't help herself – well, most racists can't, can they? Look at Trump."

"I can't look at him. I tried once. The thing she hates most about America is that everyone is a Labradoodle, a mutt."

Charlotte shrugged casually, "She expects us to cleave to Aryan purity."

"I'm going to be sick."

"Not on this rug, please."

The seating-chart conversation with Charlotte about names and race gave him the heebie-jeebies. he sipped tea and thought of ways to flee, as Charlotte pondered where to hide her cousin Claudia. Byron thought that he loved but didn't like his fiancée. On the receiving end, her renowned sarcastic put downs stung. He feared her and, as defense, employed exceptional pretending skills. By now, he feared, they had nothing in common except pretense.

Byron picked up the surprisingly oily pistol and put the barrel in his mouth. He realized now that marrying Charlotte would be a colossal mistake, yet time had run out to undo things. Twisting his hand, he imitated the angle that Jeb at the gun store said would cause instant death; Byron did not believe in instant death. He believed in brief agonizing thrashing, at best, or excruciating minutes of paralyzed suffering at worst. Further, he didn't know if Jeb had loaded the gun at the store or if Byron was meant to it at home. Guns were more complicated than he had appreciated. Contemplating now the messy magnitude of his action, he set the gun down on the pew.

With a groan, he dropped his forehead against the pew in front of him. He felt estranged from the world, utterly indifferent to everything. Byron used to worry that he felt emotions too intensely; now, he wondered if he felt them at all. Only once, that he could recollect, had he truly felt at one with the world. He had gone camping in Maine with his Aunt Olivia: woodland smells, a serene evening, a campfire, the profound darkness, and then the soothing hooves of deer walking around their tent in the morning.

He sat upright and felt the heft of the pistol. Looking up at the chapel's moldy ceiling, he saw that it had once been beautiful.

Olivia stood just inside the chapel and stared at her treasured nephew, who sat with a pistol barrel in his mouth and his finger on the trigger.

"I've got a lot of morphine stored up, honey – and it makes things a heck of a lot easier to clean up afterward."

Byron turned and looked at her but said nothing. He did not move the gun.

"Are you drunk, Sweetie?"

"Yes," he said.

"Very?"

"Perhaps."

"Well, then," she said, moving down the aisle to sit beside him. Once there, she took the gun from his mouth and placed it next to them. She rustled around in her purse, found what she was looking for, ripped off the top, and handed him a packet of caffeine-laced power powder.

He stared at it, shrugged, and then swallowed it. He gagged and spat.

"That ought to help sober you up." Olivia said, as she massaged the middle of his back. "You're meant to drink it with something sweet, like apple juice. They give those things out like candy to us cancer patients. I don't know why they think we need to stay awake, but they do."

He looked at her.

"Sitting in a dark closet staring at mops is better than dying, my love."

He shrugged.

"Trust me. I've stared at a few mops in my life, and I'd trade this," and she waggled a hand at her dying body, "for any one of them."

"I think I'm making a huge mistake."

"I believe you mean getting married, but I hope you mean putting a bullet through your head too. And you think you're making a mistake? Honey, I'd be damned sure before I blew my brains out."

"I'm sure."

"If there's one thing I've learned is that it's difficult – maybe impossible – to know which path to take in life. I've certainly taken the wrong one repeatedly."

He leaned his head on her bone-hard shoulder.

"Of course," she said, "You don't realize you've taken the wrong path until ..."

"It's too late?"

She laughed, and then winced with pain. "I was going to say until it's nearly too late."

He smiled at that. "You've had the most amazing life, working in Africa, farming on a commune in ..."

"Nova Scotia. Communes were what one did back in my day – at least for a while. Mind you, I wasn't there for any kind of communing.' She gave him a sly wink. "Lord have mercy, he was a big, broad-chested man, eyes as violet as Elizabeth Taylor's."

" I love you, Aunt Olivia."

"I love you too. So, how's about you don't blow your brains out. I think I'd rather die before you, even if it does mean you have to hot-wire your sexual engine and marry the wrong person. Sorry to be so selfish."

"The last thing you are is selfish."

"No," she said with a smile, "the last thing I am – and ever will be – is nice to your mother."

They both laughed.

"Who in the Hell invited that ragamuffin?" Virginia Wildwood demanded of her husband. Hovering in the after-vicinity of fifty, Virginia Wildwood was one of the world's most beautiful – and wealthy – women. Her perfect skin and mesmerizing gray-green eyes made her mountains of money seem almost insignificant – an evolutionary illusion that Virginia relied upon to weaken her foes.

"Byron."

"My Byron –?"

"Virginia, for the love of God – it's Olivia."

"Oh, dear."

Out of vanity, Virginia was not wearing her glasses. She had been born into one of the wealthiest families in South Africa. What she hadn't inherited she made from her magazine empire, at whose head the style magazine *Filles et Plaisir* raked in millions. It had been among the first to go digital and the hard copy remained the display rag of choice from Upper East Side townhouses to fancier cosmetic surgeons in Westchester and Fairfield Counties.

She squinted at the thin woman in a bright red ensemble. "Why's my little sister wearing a dress three sizes too big? Don't tell me she bought that thing off the rack."

Her husband's usual sigh, then, "If you ever went to visit, you would know that the chemotherapy is ruthless."

"You sound like a lawyer."

"I *am* a lawyer. Look. I know you made a vow not to speak to one another 'ever again,' which I thought at the time was idiotic, although I admit that trip to Budapest was crazy-making – but Byron has always loved her, the two of them have had a very special relationship."

"Camping up in Maine. My parents did not raise their daughters to go camping in Maine I can tell you that. Mama always said she had lesbian tendencies, didn't she?"

"What your mother said about any of us wouldn't bear repeating in a church. And what on earth is wrong with having lesbian tendencies? Or actually being lesbian?" Another familiar sigh. "I think Olivia has made a heroic effort to come here today."

"You don't go out in public when you have these sorts of – issues. She's just doing it to annoy me."

"Or because she wants to see Byron get married."

Virginia laughed. "I give that marriage – for which, thank God in Heaven, we're not paying – two months, tops."

"Yes, yes, don't repeat the whole damn thing."

"I shall repeat as I feel repeating is required. In the event you haven't noticed, our son Byron is gay."

"So, you say, and which may explain why he has bonded with your sister with the lesbian tendencies. And in the event, I hadn't noticed – and I'm not certain just what it is that one notices – then you've conveniently told me many times."

"Don't take a tone with me, Buchanan, and you certainly do know what one notices. We live in New York, for God's sake, so don't play naïve."

They stared at one another.

Satisfied, Virginia went on. "We may not be paying for this fiasco, but we're going to lose a bundle by the time it's over. They have no pre-nup. You're the lawyer. Do they have a pre-nup?"

"There is no pre-nup."

"What was Byron thinking? Is it some suicidal urge? We know why's she marrying him. I mean, besides the fact that he's adorable. Because we're rich. That's why. I'm aristocratic and famous and your family is more American than apple pie – in fact, they pre-date apple pies. They've been around looting and amassing fortunes since the mid-1600s, and that ancestral tree of yours has everything in it from gibbons to senators to murderous crooks to captains of commerce – and occasionally all in one life-time." She smiled, her way of making peace. "It's one of America's finest families." She patted his hand. A pause. "Whatever is she trying to do?"

"Who?

"Olivia, in that hideous red thing, that's hanging off her like a – what are those Hawaiian things they all wear because they're fat? Mumus?"

"I have no idea what you're talking about, but I believe Olivia is greeting people. She's always had a people personality."

"People personality," Virginia growled under her breath. Then she flagged down a groom's man. "Now, this hunk o' man – who is he? Do we know him? He looks familiar. He'd suit Byron a Hell of a lot better than – oh, hello, dear," She said to the handsome young man leaning over, "Could you do me a favor? Yes? And what's your name?"

"Sean, ma'am."

"Sean ...?"

"O'Malley."

"You were at school with Byron, I knew we recognized you. You Collegiate boys have that glow. Of course, you're six feet two inches, aren't you? You do stand out."

"Six one," he said.

"So honest. It speaks well of your mother – but mind, you needn't fudge the details. You're not five feet seven or something equally dwarfish. Temptation gets the better of men who are five feet seven. They are always going to be five feet seven *and a half.*"

She and Sean the groom's man laughed.

"Sean, if you would be so kind, could you ask that woman in red over there to sit down and stay put."

The young man glanced over and then looked back at Olivia, twisted with pain.

"And take care – she has *an odor.*"

This time the young man looked as if she had slapped him. "*Excuse me*, Mrs. Wildwood?"

"It's all the drugs she takes; they give off the smell of an oil refinery."

"*Oh, for the love of God,*" Buchanan said, loudly enough for the people behind them to hear. He stood, pushed the handsome water-polo playing groom's man aside, and went over to Olivia. He pulled her into a hug, and the two of them talked for several minutes – until, in fact, Buchanan showed her the door to the side chapel, which no one ever used after Helen Franklin, who dominated the vestry claimed it had toxic mold.

Returning to his seat he said, "She smells deliciously of Clive Christian perfume.

"How in God's name do they afford that?"

A third sigh. A long pause. Then, Buchanan asked, "Who chose these hymns? Good God, *they're from the dark ages.*"

"I chose them. And don't tell me how to be an Episcopalian, Mr. Buchanan Wildwood."

"I hadn't planned on it. However, I've tended to think of you as a more forward-thinking woman than "All Glory Laud and Honor to Thee Redeemer King" would imply.

"*Oh*," she said in surprise. "Well, you do have your moments, Nate." She stared a moment at the assembled wedding guests. "Nate, this unseemly spectacle. We need to talk."

"About what?"

"Of many things: Of shoes – and ships – and sealing-wax – Of cabbages – and kings – And why the sea is boiling hot – And whether pigs have wings."

"But wait a bit – the Oysters cried, before we have our chat; for some of us are out of breath –"

"I believe the next line is 'And all of us are fat,'" Virginia said with a quick smile, "So perhaps we should leave off our little literary allusion there, Mr. Smarty Pants."

"All right," Nate said. "But I love 'The Walrus and the Carpenter.' It's from *Alice through the Looking-Glass*, though I prefer 'Jabberwocky'."

"I have no opinion on this matter," she shrugged. "It's never yet been necessary to have one. Is it necessary, do you think?"

"I suppose not."

"And you know full well what we need to talk about." She gave him one of her take-no-prisoners looks. "About our gay son marrying a woman, for starters." Then, looking across the church she said in mock horror, "Surely, they haven't invited *those* girls. I mean, honestly. They've gone too far. Those girls should stay indoors and write poetry, like Emily Dickinson – or else, much more sensibly, have their faces done over with cosmetic surgery. I've said as much to her mother." She sighed. "I mean, it's not as if they *can't afford it.* And what kind of Upper East Side mother lets her daughters go through life looking like Godzilla? I ask you?"

In one of the few quiet moments in the ceremony, gunshots reverberated from the side chapel. Charlotte screamed and the fleeing Priest tripped over his vestments. Byron, intuiting the cause, leapt toward the chapel, followed by a few of his hardier groomsmen. For years, the chapel had been a refuge of crumbling statuary. When he opened the door, Byron faced a row of statues with their crotches blown off, puffing moldy plaster powder from their mutilated crotches. As others attempted to decipher the gruesome mystery, Byron noticed a stylish high heel in the aisle, and discovered where his Aunt Olivia, suffering with cancer, had stripped off her clothes before injecting herself with morphine and shooting the offending statues. She lay naked now in death, a needle, and its syringe in her arm below a rubber band.

As quickly as possible, Byron gathered up the morphine bottles, tucked them in his various pockets, took out the needle and syringe, cleaned away the small bit of blood from Olivia's arm, and then slipped those in another pocket. He cut through the rubber band with his nail clippers, which he placed in his lapel pocket. Picking up the red dress with its designer label, he carefully covered her up. The pistol lay on the floor. That he left behind.

"*What* ...?" Charlotte asked, standing in full regalia in the doorway, her red-faced father behind her.

"My Aunt just killed herself," Byron said. Then he turned to one of his friends, who examined the blasted crotches, "Bruce, would fetch my Uncle Cyril."

CHAPTER

2

Windows down, headset tied securely in place by a loop of twine, Sandrine Ducos belted out the lyrics of Mylène Farmer's *"Elle à dit."* She swerved on to the narrow highway shoulder, punched her Volkswagen to 110 kilometers per hour, avoided a decomposed wheel rim, grazed the concrete barrier, and then rocketed in front of a hulking two-trailered Carrefour Supermarket truck, all without missing a beat. However, not before her ageing car let loose a flatulent explosion of black smoke.

Through a combination of scheming, conspiring and cut-throatery, Sandrine Ducos had bought the three most lucrative coin-operated Laundromats in Lyon. *"Mais je n'ai rien foutre,"* her favorite expression, usually blew out behind the cigarette in the corner of her mouth. It translated into English as, "I couldn't give a fuck." She was on the way to stay with her son Laurent and his American husband Alex. Having a gay son amounted to a badge of honor in the districts in which Sandrine's laundries were situated. In fact, she credited camera-friendly Laurent and handsome Alex's visits (one summer day she forced Alex to take his shirt off and sit outside in his hairy-chested splendor) with increasing her business at *Place Louis Pradel* by 43.67%.

Sandrine had been born mathematically gifted, a fact that mischievous employees discovered only at the moment of their dismissal – when faced by a dossier of proof, stamped by the *notaire* from the applicable ministry, fulfilling the convoluted legal requirements for firing someone in France.

She had promised Laurent and Alex that she would reach their house by 14h30 and she was already half an hour late. Traffic on the A10 had hindered even crafty Sandrine, who knew every means of dodging traffic jams: driving on the other side of the road, off-roading through the back gardens of traumatized middle-class families, across fields and through death-defying woodlands. Once, she made it across the tarmac of a rural airport in front of a plane, when it was indispensable that she get to a cousin's wedding.

On Kitty-Louise Calhoun's only visit to her son Alex's home in France she suffered a sudden and fatal heart attack before entering the front door. Her last words were, "*So*, looks like the big-spender boys got themselves some new ..." and then nature did its magic. Alex guessed she was commenting on their double-glazed windows or the oak door and knocker. As his husband Laurent pointed out, homophobic Kitty-Louse would have chosen whatever hurt Alex most. His mother knew that Alex always rose to Laurent's defense, so bets were on the obviously Laurent-purchased knocker and door.

On exiting her car and seeing a dead foreign woman on the walkway, Sandrine grasped why an irksome Coroner's van had obstructed her way since the turn off from the A10 – causing her twice to stick her head out and hurl obscenities. She had pulled into Alex and Laurent's driveway behind the coroner and quickly established herself as a first-rate assistant, chiefly because – as she made clear from the start – she wanted Madame's shoes and skirt – and what Sandrine wanted, Sandrine got.

It proved more difficult to get Kitty-Louise *out* of Godiche village than into it. In fact, the entire village ended up involved, with even *Monsieur le Maire* helping decipher the forms, which demanded detailed information about patrimony and a *notaire* to take inventory of her clothes and possessions, which meant three suitcases and a large tote bag purse – and, of course, her wig. The Gendarmes stashed Kitty's corpse in a meat locker at the Carrefour hypermarket in Fontenay-le-Comte, since Godiche had no facilities for a long-term layover.

Kitty-Louise might have spent eternity in her meat locker, had an efficient woman named Tesla not appeared from the Consulate in Bordeaux – and with ruthless vigor sorted things out within *hours*. As Laurent said, in the politically incorrect way of the French, "If you need something done in France, hire a lesbian – and if it's an especially tough business, get a Jewish lesbian." Tesla was efficient, though no one asked if she fit Laurent's criteria. She seemed to conform to gender neutral terminology and she had no visible religious paraphernalia. Stereotypical appearances were good enough in rural France; assumptions were truth. Tesla stumped the system.

Alex and Laurent fell silent in awe, as they listened to her on the phone wrestling a bureaucrat into the metaphorical mud. Thanks to Tesla, Kitty-Louise was trucked from the meat locker, where they had been lodged between frozen chicken livers and microwave dinners, burned to ash, bone bits crushed, remains boxed, wrapped and shipped off to the States. Being a Vegan, Tesla refused their offer for dinner, gave them requisite double-cheek kisses, and sped off in her Renault Clio – the car that Laurent always referred to as *le clitoris des voitures*, which might have pleased Tesla had she lingered long enough to hear clitoris spoken with a French accent.

"She has heard it hundreds of times I am sure," Laurent said with his Gallic logic, "She makes lesbianism, yes?"

"We say 'She *is* a Lesbian' in English."

"I see," Laurent pondered the matter a moment. "But what is the difference?"

Alex burst out laughing and grabbed Laurent in a bear hug.

Later that evening, Sandrine stood at the window in her favorite guest room and watched the sunset over the Vendée. Behind her, she heard music from the speakers she had installed on arrival. It was the same music the gay crowd listened to at her Laundromats. Gay men were excellent customers: respectful, clean, no scuff marks and they always separated their whites from colors. She loved the song that played now. Of course, she didn't know any English, but nonetheless she blew a puff of smoke and swayed slightly to her favorite. She was savoring her victory over the *notaire* in obtaining the new shoes and skirt from off Kitty-Louise's corpse, moments before the municipality trucked it over to the crematorium. In fact, the navy-blue skirt fluttered now in her window, an advertisement to the village that she had scored one on the bureaucracy.

Beating the bureaucracy came second only to soccer as France's national sport.

To Alex's mind, few places achieved the beauty of France's Vendée Province at sunset. He loved how it spread out in its river valley, sun bursting on brown, beige, and white, a blue-green river passing beneath Napoleonic bridges, past monuments to glory, and beside the melon fields that had made the Province rich. On this sunny summer evening, Alex jogged shirtless on the path leading to the river. As he ran, he thought about his mother's sudden and ghastly death as he listened to music, his favorite, a Country Western song with memories of a time and a man, the Maverick's iconic "Oh, What a Crying Shame."

Of course, to have anyone die in front of you would be shocking; even more so when it is your mother, it ... well, that's where Alex's thinking hit a wall. He had not liked his mother. Nonetheless, she was the women who gave him life and some small part of him hoped for a reconciliation. Maybe. Truthfully, and perhaps embarrassingly, he was more upset by the ghastly circumstances of her death than he was by her death itself. Shouldn't he be grieving more? Was he even grieving?

He paused and thought. But all he thought about was how she clutched her breast with a pained screechy noise, and then the crazy aftermath. It felt like a story you told over beers with friends and everyone laughed. Sure, it was tragic; but it was comically tragic. However, all of that aside, shouldn't he be mourning? Wouldn't most people be crying? He did not have the smallest urge to cry over his mother's death. She had been a hard and judgmental woman, often unkind and rarely loving. Well then.

Alex stood up straight: athletic, with gym-perfect pectorals, a flat stomach, and a hairy chest. He kept a permanent five o'clock shadow, which he stroked a moment as he began again to run. He was, after all, a self-made man who lived in France. This was not a man his mother could ever have created; it was not a man his mother could ever really have loved. As he came up to the river, he turned left and ran along the top of the embankment.

When he reached his evening spot, he leaned over to catch his breath and then he stood peaceably on the bank of the Vendée River, watching the descending sun glint off the water as it gurgled over stones and through the reeds. Grey-blue shadows intensified into green woodlands and melon fields, silhouettes spread into trees, grew branches, and let loose chattering flocks of scarlet and white birds. 'Life has either too much or too little meaning," he thought.

Reflecting on his French husband Laurent, who hated ambiguity of that sort, he smiled. Alex had never met anyone so lovingly confusingly self-contradictory. He smiled again thinking about his friends back in Sioux City, Iowa, where he had grown up. "Most of them must think I'm completely nuts – and maybe I am," he thought. The truth was that he had found something here with Laurent that had always been missing.

If that made him nuts; so be it.

Alex's grandmother claimed that having twin girls came as a surprise. However, Woodbury County prided itself on her talent for lying – sending her once to speak to a Federal official nosing around into farm subsidies, and then throwing a party for her when the man left with promises of more money for more mythical sorghum. So, Alex surmised that – neither surprised, nor caught off guard – she had planned months before the event to split the name she had chosen for a girl.

One twin was christened Louise-Katherine and the other Katherine-Louise, or as they came to be known, the Kitties, since one took the moniker Kitty-Louise and the other Louise-Kitty. People often reported seeing the Kitties at the Chicken Hut or at Walmart, even though they strove for different identities. They even chose separate Episcopal Churches, after Kitty-Louise claimed that the female priest at St. Clément's touched her breasts during communion. As Laurent said, "How did she find them?" Neither sister had an ample bosom – though ample attitude, by way of compensation.

Attitude without reason was a Sioux City specialty. Big boobs, good looks and money mattered in Sioux City. Though he had mocked Sioux City in his youth, from the vantage point of life in France, Alex felt he finally understood his hometown. France taught Alex to look kindlier on the need to hide insecurity behind pretense. In France, keeping face trumped education, political position, and money – especially money. Haughty waiters who felt superior to her purse full of Euros would have been befuddled Kitty-Louise, had she lived long enough, by or – had they known – her expensive wig.

In one of those synchronous twin happenings one reads about, the sisters had their one and only child a month apart. Of course, since the two families lived in big-yard, back-to-back Victorian houses, with a permanently unlatched gate – except for that seven-month period in which the sisters weren't speaking, due to a disagreement over their mother's coffin being open or closed during the viewing.

Passionately upbeat, Lizzy saw the concealed benefit in every dark cloud – including tornadoes: "Oh, hell's bells, those were the *ugliest* damned houses in the county." In response to the seventeen reported deaths, she chirped, "We all must go sometime, don't we? I'd rather be killed in a tornado than be eaten alive by cancer." She got straight A grades in school and scored so high on the mandated IQ test that the district sent her off to Des Moines, where a new test enhanced her score by twenty points.

Lizzy could quote entire passages from classic authors. She would pipe up with Dickens to Virgil to the Marquis de Sade, depending – obviously – upon the event. Alex loved her as one loves a dog that bites or a splintery but otherwise decent screen door. Alex found her at the foot of his bed one summery Saturday morning, waking to her chipper observation that, "You've got yourself a prize-winning zucchini of a boner, Cuz."

He often found her unexpectedly at their dinner table. Lizzie would be chattering away about flooding in Bangladesh and the effects of rising ocean levels in Vanuatu. Sometimes she went trilling away with observations everyone went on eating around her, "As Henry James said, 'Experience is never limited, and it is never complete; it is an immense sensibility, a kind of huge spiderweb of the finest silken threads suspended in the chamber of consciousness and catching every airborne particle in its tissue'." However, alone in his family, Lizzy supported him when he came out, and for that he gave her eternal bonus points.

Alex's coming out had become countywide folklore. As a rule, the Sioux City wealthier set, kept such events as comings out quiet – however, unfortunately for Sioux City Society, the Calhoun's were incapable of being quiet on any subject, let alone gay rights. Alex had chosen what he *thought* was a perfect moment; they had eaten Christmas dinner, with both sisters and their husbands and Lizzy all together, sprawled about the living room soothingly liquored up.

However, the *Calhoun Situation* – as the Woodbury Country Club dubbed it – did not go as planned. Alex made his short, eloquent announcement, briefly quoting Dr. Ruth – and then both sisters screamed in what Lizzy called "Rocky Horror Picture Show style" and fainted – although they crumpled into suspiciously comfortable positions on the Calhoun's thick Persian carpet.

The two fathers flew off with curses, followed by Alex's father launching Alex's baseball trophy through the living window, roaring over the smashing glass, "You won't want this anymore." His uncle took a milder path – being a guest in the house, after all – of throwing his whiskey tumbler into the fireplace, with the shout, "If he's turned Lizzy into a lesbian, I'm latching that fucking gate until *Hell freezes over.*"

For her part, Lizzy – while clapping her hands and periodically whistling with two fingers – leapt around the room, over the sisters and broken glass from the window through which the baseball trophy had been projected, squawking, "How exciting, how amazing, oh, *wow*, my oh my, my very own gay cousin, isn't this just *fantastic,* Muffin?"

In the foggy beginnings of time, Alex earned the nickname Muffin. Various theories as to its origin had come and gone, but Kitty-Louise remained ever furious about people referring to her son by the same name, "As some big haired woman's *Chihuahua.*" For most of his life, Alex had treasured his moniker.

However, in close juxtaposition he moved from having his first long-term boyfriend screaming shirtless from their fourth-floor dorm room – in what might kindly be called a girlish trill – "*Muffy-poo,*" to living with a beautiful Frenchman whose mouth could only say something that rhymed with Loofah, the French 'u' being one of those sounds foreigner's never master and Frenchmen never lose. Fortunately, Laurent proved more trainable than Jerad and they settled on Alex.

Laurent self-identified as a tribute to the appalling state of French public education. He claimed that he had learned more French grammar from Alex than all his *Profs* combined. When first together, lying cozily in bed under a fluffy duvet on a Winter's night, Alex would regale Laurent with French history, about which Laurent's ignorance made enthralled by the Battle of Agincourt; and by Napoleon's farewell address to his loyal officers from the stairs of Fontainebleau Palace.

That story made Laurent cry; a charming trait at the time, but one that Alex ultimately found irritating and tried – unsuccessfully – to curtail. Beautiful Laurent once burst into tears of joyful happiness as he told Alex that he loved him because was not as beautiful as he was virile. In the Laurent hierarchy, virile outranked simple beauty. Laurent cried at everything: dead badgers to a story on the evening news about a container of suffocated parrots in Marseilles.

Sleeves rolled up, shirt unbuttoned, Laurent stood in the farthest corner of their garden, where the oaks grew thickest, and the shadows were cool. He lifted his face toward ripening fields. Laurent, in his French fashion, had always suspicioned the Anglo-Saxon tendency to romanticize landscape, and yet here he had discovered enchantment in the mauve streaks of setting sun touching uncut hay and swollen grain; landscape as Zola wrote it and Monet painted it.

Though well advanced the evening sun seemed reluctant to loosen its hold. A balmy breeze embraced him. Flowers drooped in the tall grass; their scents flushed out by the moist heat. Their terrier, Beowulf, only just emerged from the taxing throes of puppyhood, slept heavily beneath the apple tree. Birds fluttered overhead.

Laurent thought it time he and Beowulf went looking for the man of their lives, that endearingly daft – but virile – American named Alex whom both Laurent and Beowulf loved dearly. When he made a clicking noise, Beowulf leapt to his feet. Together they walked over the lawn to the patio and then out across the melon fields toward the river.

Laurent had, of course, snooped at Alex's playlist and had fallen in love with a strangely beautiful Country Western song, "Oh, What a Crying Shame," by the Mavericks. As he and Beowulf walked through an oak grove toward the banks of the Vendée, his mind on his handsome husband, he was unaware that he whistled the song.

'One of the troubles with living out in the country," Laurent thought, "is that you quested for different and better music, nicer bistros and sexier men." Of course, most older people thought that Fontenay-le-Comte, their nearest big city was wonderful. Laurent bent down to pet Beowulf. Alex spoke on the phone last night with one of his American friends, and their conversation troubled Laurent.

Laurent gave his all into turning Alex into a *proper Frenchman*, and then these American friends filled his head his stupid Anglo-Saxon notions. As Laurent told Alex afterward, when he dared brag about his friend Tom's promotion, "A job is just a means to an end, it simply can't be your passion – unless your job was musical or literary, artistic in some fashion."

After a testy conversation on the subject, Laurent concluded by saying, "I think I've had more moments of insight sitting there playing the piano than any other place on earth – and that, dear Alex, is why work is a pain in the ass."

CHAPTER

3

Lizzie had always wanted to do it and tonight she did.

She stripped down naked, including for the first time before showering or swimming, her panties (though not her phone and earbuds), opened the French doors in the dining room and ran across the grass, through the leafy, big-mansion streets of The Heights, Sioux City Iowa's old money address. At first, she felt liberated, freed in a fashion she had only ever imagined. However, having to look out for icky things made cross walks a nuisance. Whenever possible, she kept to the grassy areas – though they had their own canine perils.

As she ran naked through the streets of The Heights, she listened to the Mavericks, singing her favorite song, "Oh, what a Crying Shame," and then she started crying as she thought about – well, *too many things to hold in one blizzard of tears.*

Lizzie recalled how, at the age of fourteen, after her first full week of Ninth Grade, she had sat outside watching the starry sky and considering the week just past. She had eaten dinner at her rich cousin Alex's house (an identical clapboard surrounded by chestnut trees, one street behind their own, connected by a gate in the fence). Her rich and independent-school educated cousin Alex had a snappy Great Gatsby vocabulary and a trajectory to the top of American society mapped out by hired classroom whores and behind-the scenes heavy lifting. Alex had gone to an Episcopal day school in the chic neighborhood of Gilman Terrace, and later to the best private school in town.

Lizzie's parents thought such private schooling worthlessly snobby, without understanding that in America only snobby people, crooks, cheats, braggarts and pompous fools actually get ahead in life – proudly sent their daughter Lizzie to Sioux City's antiquated public schools, including a high school that actually bragged that 79.4% of the students graduated.

No one knew what the .4% stood for until Lizzie managed to explain – at least to those in her homeroom – that it was merely a mathematical average and not a real number at all – for all they knew 100% graduated last year and 25% this year. Her classmates did not applaud her explanation.

That night, at the age of fourteen, the parts of the conversation that hit Lizzie the hardest skimmed right over her parents' heads; However, Lizzie felt truly walloped. What she learned that night was existential; it altered her life. Lizzie understood that, unlike her cousin with his sassy-classy uniform, Lacrosse stick, slick new editions of classic novels, and state of the art science labs, as a public-school child in Iowa, wearing her trash-talk street clothes, Lizzie and her fellow students were a litter of piglets wallowing in pedagogical mud. Even if she aced every Honors and AP Course, took at least two languages, and – *well* – got an A in everything, she would still not have a diploma that an Ivy League would look at twice.

Unless she managed to stumble into that coveted (but rare) "geographic diversity" quota, or she filled in the SAT bubbles saying she was a Mung tribeswoman or crippled Russian orphan – she was toast. As her chipper public-school advisor in her Walmart pant suit told her in their first meeting, "You're a snap for State, Liz" and seeing Lizzie's scowl said, "There's nothing wrong with State." A long glaring look of animosity before Lizzie said (remembering all too well the luxurious bubble of her cousin's academia), "Until you have to acknowledge that it's run and operated by the *State of Iowa.*"

In addition to the existential conversation, Lizzie had looked at Alex's 'Program of Study' that evening, which had thoroughly irked her, with its mouth-watering electives and selectives (as if his seasonal two-outfit uniform had not already made her seethe with envy). She also overheard her aunt talking about his once-a-year fancy pants school trip to Europe from Ninth Grade in St. Petersburg to Rome to London and then senior year in Paris. Lizzie would be lucky to get a spot on their January school trip – once every other year – to Quebec City at the height of winter, Quebec being to winter as summer was to Tucson.

Such was the life of her cousin Alex, the pampered only son of parents with the fashion sense of long-haul truckers but plenty of money – at least by Sioux City standards. They stood for the American Dream: truckers who produce doctors who in turn produce drifters and drug addicts. Even as a child, in a wet and windy Iowa winter, her cousin Alex – who she was off soon to see in in France, where he lived with his French husband Laurent – never looked mussed. In summer, flies landed on *her* by the – whatever you called a herd of flies – but not on him. In spring, his shoes never muddied. His bicycle remained as clean after ten years of use as the day his grandparents bought it for him. At school, his homework invariably came in the neatest. He easily won every debate championship; he was both Captain of the Baseball Team and the stalwart lead in *The Pirates of Penzance*.

Alex's beauty, indigo eyes, and a fluffy oriole of sexy hair, had always allowed him to wear clothes well. People ogled Alex in jeans and a tank top at the grocery store and at the Sioux City Opera in evening wear. Lizzie imagined that in France he now had closets full of clothes of every conceivable sort, all of which he wore well.

So, Lizzie ran naked through the streets of Sioux City, Iowa, listening to The Mavericks, cursing her cousin, and crying her eyes out, screaming, "*I fucking hate the fucking goddamned world*," and crying all the harder and screaming all the louder as lights popped on in bedroom windows. As it was, she had to climb back up into her room via the chestnut tree in the backyard, since someone had already picked up her clothes. At least she had the rest of the night to think up a plausible excuse for leaving her panties on the lawn – which she did.

Everything had gone wrong with Lizzy's trip. Her Uncle Luther was taking his annual hunting trip to Western Australia, where Kangaroos made shooting them a major party by dint of their stupidity. They bumbled straight at the guns, or leapt into each other, and once – according to a well-told tale – into someone's house through the back door, hopping out through the front door. He had stored his packed suitcases at Lizzy's house, so he could go to Des Moines for his friend Ted's birthday, since he didn't, "Trust that shifty character Kitty-Louise hired to feed the dogs."

Therefore, Lizzy, who had the same matching cases bought in a bulk purchase at Walmart, discovered that Uncle Luther had gone to Perth with her size 6-summer ensemble and she had her Uncle's XL Big and Tall collection of winter hunting wear. She made the discovery through happenstance when her right shoe broke and, while retrieving a new pair of shoes, found only a pair of size eleven men's hunting boots.

Dipping into her travel budget, she purchased a pair of sandals from a cart and then – for reasons unknown – she actually checked the bags despite the uselessness of Old Spice after shave, polyester fleece jackets, and a stash of well-worn copies of *Tit and Tuck*, delivered monthly to a P.O. Box out in Eastwood Junction.

Once on board the plane in Chicago, things grew worse. An elderly Frenchwoman had taken Lizzy's seat and refused to budge, pointing Lizzy toward her abandoned window seat in the last row of Business Class. Flying Business had been a treat Lizzy gave herself. Half a year ago she had reserved her front-row aisle seat, to which she had been guided by Seat Guru: First to be fed going east, first off the plane, most legroom – all of which the back-window seat had in reverse.

She remembered that it was red on Seat Guru, meaning never take this seat no matter what, and now the airline insisted she *sit there*. She'd be stuck eating fish or something vegetarian, would have to climb over someone to go to the toilet, and left to scramble out toward immigration with what Aunt Kitty Louise always called "The cattle."

For a while, Lizzy held her own in this French-language argument, possessing a fluency (from years of study) that proved as useless in Sioux City as apparently it did on the airplane, since the Senior Attendant intervened to demand that Lizzy relinquish her seat to "*Madame*," since *Madame* was elderly. To make it more distressing, as Lizzy protested that she had reserved the seat months ago for her first ever visit to France, all the French people glared at her as if *she* were the nuisance. Only when the six-foot three Purser appeared and told her that she would be put off the plane if she did not "*behave*," did she relent and move to the spot that Seat Guru had given the red X of doom.

The seat was as terrible as Seat Guru predicted, and the creature next to her – of unknown gender and ethnicity, wearing filthy multi-colored robes and head gear – could kindly be called obese and smelled as if he or she had not bathed in months. Ripping the cellophane off her travel diary with repressed fury, Lizzy at once wrote on the cover, "The Trip from Hell." She'd never written the word Hell before, so it had a reckless thrill to it.

She described her companion in Hell as Jabba the Hut, since he or she draped over the seat arm like oozing jelly as it slept – reeking and snoring like a Harley Davidson. Lizzy ate her cold vegetable lasagna (gluten free), and indignantly accepted half a glass of the dregs from the last Merlot bottle. She even cried briefly when, trying to climb over Jabba the Hut to go to the toilet, she fell into the aisle and banged her head on a woman's seat who, awakened from slumber, lifted her eye mask and said to her husband in French, "That difficult American woman *again.*"

After begging for a glass of water from an attendant who pretended not to hear her, she finally burst out in unheard-of Lizzy wrath, using every French curse word she knew. She did get better service after that, though considering that she couldn't even put her food tray out flat due to Jabba's bulk, it supplied no real comfort. By the time she arrived at Charles de Gaulle, she was no longer Lizzy – she had transmogrified into someone else. In the predicted mêlée at immigration where – because of the impenetrable barrier of Jabba, she was the *only* Business Class passenger without a priority pass – she struggled through the hordes. When she discovered that she had missed her scheduled train to Niort, she surrendered to another bout of French swearing, and sent a terse text to her cousin Alex and his French husband Laurent:

Fucking flight from Hell and missed the fucking train. Liz

She sat sullenly on her luggage for forty-five minutes, prophesying that the TGV would be as enormous a debacle as everything else – including the fact that she now wore men's size 40 Levi's, hitched up by a belt with a silver kangaroo buckle, a flannel shirt and hunting boots, the front two-thirds of which were stuffed with Uncle Luther's polyester blend socks. Her ensemble caused everyone to stare at her, as if she were an eccentric painter or famous lesbian poet. She had to wear the outfit because, as she made her awkward way down the stairs to the TGV station, she slipped and fell into a mossy, debris-filled mini-lake where a portion of the concrete platform had subsided.

When the next train finally arrived, the conductor accepted her ticket. However, without an assigned seat she spent thirty minutes having officious people move her around from car to car until, at last, she found refuge in a solo seat next to a toilet. She had never been unhappier, more wearied, annoyed, or dismayed.

She relented and smiled at the cute Steward who sold her a little sandwich and a miniature cup of roofing-tar coffee – though the way he regarded her was rather as she had regarded Jabba, as someone distastefully odd. A cute Frenchman's disdain, when she *knew* she'd have had him flirting up a storm if she were wearing her low-cut sun dress, only made her more – *what*? Was there even a *word* for it? Desolate? Dejected? Thinking of her lost belongings, she ate her dry little sandwich through her tears.

Lizzy looked up from the magazine she'd bought in Chicago, since her collected novels had also traveled to the Outback with Uncle Tom, as a young backpack man slumped to the floor, virtually at her feet. His hair had blond too-much-sun highlights and sprouted in ways unintended by the stylist, since Lizzy discerned the remnants of a fashionable haircut. He smelled like the boys at summer camp; his body odor had cleanliness underneath it, as if at some point he had showered and used deodorant. Athletes smelled like that when they rushed sweating through the halls. She watched him for a while, and then decided she ought to say something about his proximity to the toilet.

"*Monsieur, je fais mes excuses, mais je crois que vous devriez savoir que vous êtes –*" she had said, when the young man looked up.

The suntanned face with bright green eyes, despite the fact that it hadn't been shaved in days, unmistakably belonged to Dalton Countryman, the most popular boy in her high school – with whom she had been on greeting terms, but nothing more. Clearly, he had been crying. Tears stains streaked down his face. They regarded one another, as he began to puzzle her face out, and while she said, "*Dalton?*" he said, "*Lizzy?*"

"*What ...?*" They both said at once.

Then, "Kandy dumped me," he said. "I mean, like, *permanently*. You know, we've been together since Sophomore year in High School – and then she met this French guy, and ..." he closed his eyes and struggled not to cry, "decided to stay with him in Poitiers – like in his apartment, I mean – you know, his bed," and then he did sniffle a bit.

"Fuck," Lizzy said, "what a bitch."

"Tell me about it," he said, regarding Lizzy with a look he'd never given her before – one of greater respect. "The fucking disrespectful little bitch. I even bought her ticket and everything – well; my dad did, but still – huh? It wasn't even a suitable time for me take time off work – I'm in public relations with a company in Chicago – but I did it for her. The cunt." Then he looked up quickly, to see if he had gone too far. He had not.

Lizzy nodded knowingly, touching her hideous flannel shirt, under which she had been sweating profusely. "Life's a bitch. My fucking uncle took my suitcases and I got stuck with this cheap-ass crap – and my flight was a fucking nightmare, and I missed my goddamned train and ended up here," and her finger waggled with anger at the toilet door, "by that stinking goddamned toilet."

They looked at each other and nodded commiserating.

"I like your hair like that," he said.

"Oh," she reached up and touched her ponytail, a redesign demanded by her immersion in the mossy pool. "I fell in some god-awful marsh, right there on the fucking platform – and this was pretty much all I could do with it."

"Shit," he said, shaking his head. "Anyway, I like it. Makes your face stand out."

She nodded her thanks, since it was a nice compliment, but she remained fully aware of the fact that she looked like Hell.

"I shouldn't tell you this," he said, closing his eyes and staring blindly up at the ceiling, "but she was the only chick I've ever been with." He promptly put his face into his hands and sobbed.

When he simmered down, Lizzy asked, "Why shouldn't you tell me that?"

He looked at her a long while. "I don't know. It's not, like, the – well, the kind of thing you tell a girl."

"Why not?"

"I don't know. You just don't. It's not very manly, I guess."

"Oh, fuck that shit," Lizzy said with a bitter laugh. "I'll up you one Dalton. I'm a fucking goddamned virgin."

"*For real?*"

"You want to perform an examination?"

He flushed scarlet beneath his tan.

"Trust me," she said with a shrug. Her uncle's flannel itched far more than it should. Lizzy wore flannel jammies all winter long and even when brand new, they hadn't itched like this. She scouted around the bottom of the ugly green and neon blue plaid monstrosity until she found the tag. "Jesus fucking Christ. Even this piece of shit is sixty percent polyester."

He laughed.

She looked at him in surprise; he looked back at her in greater surprise. A long and genial quiet rested between them.

"Life's a bitch, huh?" he said. "Pretty girl like you still a virgin."

"I did give a blowjob to a visiting baseball player from some idiot Christian school, back in senior year, but he had to give me instructions, and I don't know how much the ordinary guy comes but that Baptist asshole poured about three gallons of his fundamentalist stuff down my throat. I was too full even to eat dinner that night."

"You haven't seen anything, honey," he said with a laugh. "I'm a fucking fire hose."

"Bragger."

"Kandy never swallowed; I always had to pull out at the last minute."

"Such a fucking sorostitute prissy ass thing to do," Lizzy said with true disdain. Why even have a boyfriend if you were going to make him shoot all over the room or drapes or ceiling? Then, thinking about it, she asked, "Where are you going, anyway?"

He shrugged and again his eyes filled with tears.

"Well, where'd you buy your ticket to?"

"I don't know. I just pointed at the arriving TGV and the guy sold me some fucking expensive ticket."

She watched him, this fellow victim of life's mean-spirited bile. "Shit. Look. Come with me, Dalton," she said.

"Where are you going?"

"To stay with my cousin Alex and his husband. Their house is huge, I mean as in three or four stories at least. It's fucking enormous, in some village in the absolute middle of goddamned nowhere – though you can drive to La Rochelle and the beach in about half an hour."

He seemed to be considering it.

"Do you have a problem with gays?" she asked.

"Hell no," he said, visibly shocked. "Shit, I love gay guys. The best blowjob I ever had was from this gay guy at a frat party. Jesus, *he* didn't need any instructions and, yes ma'am, he swallowed and liked it."

Lizzy couldn't help but laugh. "Sorry, it's just that all Alex and Laurent ever talk about is their decorations and furniture and clothes. That said,

I've always imagined that Laurent must be a pistol in bed."

"Maybe," Dalton said, with a peculiar look on his face.

She thought about his expression, which seemed suddenly deep and distant. It was indecipherable.

"Sure," he said, looking away from her, as if aware that he'd shown too much. "I'll stay."

"*Oh*. Cool. I'm sure they'll loan us their car, they're quite easy with stuff like that. I should warn you though that my god-awful Aunt Kitty-Louise will be there, and she's one rat's ass crazy country club bitch."

Again, Dalton laughed. "Know the type. So – they really wouldn't mind?"

"Trust me, Dalton. They'll talk your ear off. They love studly straight guys; it's a gay thing."

"Yeah, I've heard about that." Then after a strangely long pause he said, "You think I'm studly?"

"Why do you ask like that? I mean, Jesus, you're the all-American poster boy for a total and complete stud."

He thought about it, closing his eyes again. Then he said, "Hard to explain, Liz, but I've never seen myself that way."

"Good God. Well, it's classic. Kandy kept you under control," Lizzy said. "It's a time-honored bitch thing. My mom and aunt both do it; they

keep their men feeling inadequate and sub-
servient."

"Shit. *For real?*"

"Sunshine, hoes like Kandy and my mom
and aunt, they fucking rule the world. It's the
Nancy Reagan syndrome."

He looked puzzled.

"Never mind," she said, remembering that
History was among the subjects with which Dalton
had struggled. "Just take my word on it."

"Okay," he said. Then, "I mean, okay, I'll stay
with your cousin and his husband."

After an interminable trip in a filthy taxi
with a chain-smoking driver, who got lost at least
ten times, once nearly plunging them into a canal
covered with shamrock-colored algae, they pulled
into Alec and Laurent's drive. As they stepped out,
the driver named his exorbitant price,

Lizzy exploded in expletive-laced French
that somehow ranged from the man, his cab, the
weather, former President Sarkozy's refusal to visit
the Normandy memorial, but circled back around
to the absolute limit she intended to pay. Dalton
stood by her side, his arm over her shoulder in
what he meant to be a comforting gesture (and it
was), but surely looked to anyone watching as the

behavior of a boyfriend. Lizzy hadn't even noticed Sandrine, Alex, and Laurent approaching them across the well-tended *pelousse* bordered by towering chestnut trees.

Sandrine, the first to arrive, listened to Lizzy's French profanity, smiled, turned back toward approaching Laurent and Alex, and said through a cloud of smoke, "I fucking love this woman," at which time she promptly leapt into the argument, accusing the driver of being a crook.

Dalton removed his arm from Lizzy's shoulder, and held his hand out to Laurent and Alex. "Hi," he said. "I'm Dalton. Lizzy kind of like – you know – invited me to stay."

Alex and Laurent, having wondered about this Adonis standing there with Lizzy – no one had ever disputed Lizzy's natural beauty, which she had now disguised with a particularly quirky wardrobe. Beauty inevitably trumped weird costumes, so no one could be surprised at Lizzy successfully snagging a hunk-of-man like this – even with her Hee-Haw rancher pants and a flannel shirt.

Laurent took his hand, "*Enchanté.* I am called Laurent."

Alex followed after, "Welcome, Dalton. I'm Alex." He hooked his thumb in the direction of the argument. "What's all that?"

"Well," Dalton said, "my French isn't up to much – sorry," he offered to Laurent, who gave a Gallic shrug of indifference, "but I think it's about the price."

Laurent went over, took the driver aside, spoke a moment or two with him, and paid him. The man leapt into his vehicle and reversed down the drive so fast that appearing on the narrow farm road he came within inches of colliding with a combine harvester. This led to another argument, but far enough away to be of no concern to the group in front of the house.

"Lizzy," Alex said, pulling her into a hug, and noting that Sandrine still held her hand. "How the heck are you?"

"Shitty. Dirty. Fucked up. Goddamned bitch of a trip, except for Dalton – so far he's been the only good part."

The intense silence that followed her remarks felt like the moment before the end of the world. Birds fell silent. The wind carried the arguing farmer and cabbie's voices away across the neighboring melon field.

Sandrine pulled Lizzy closer, kissed her, and said, "Don't give a fuck about it, *Cherie*. Shit. Huh?"

"*Lizzy?*" Alex said.

"What?"

The ensuing suspension hissed with potential words, phrases, and shrieks of dismay, but all Alex finally managed to say was, "You're – you know – different."

CHAPTER

4

"I need to talk," Alex said, in French.

"But how did you know I was awake?" Laurent asked, snuggling up against Alex.

"Sleeping people make more noise, for one thing. You haven't rustled your blanket, coughed, burped, or banged the pillow in half an hour."

"You've been listening to me think."

"Which is ever so much nicer than listening to you snore – mostly."

"Why are we having this midnight vigil?"

Alex wondered about that.

"Of course," Laurent said, sounding very French, "There is always too much to think about in today's world. In ten years, the seashore shall be nipping at our stone wall."

"A hundred years."

"In earth terms," Laurent said, "There is no difference."

'It's always seems like there is more to avoid thinking about than actually to think about."

"Like apologizing? You hurt my feelings tonight," he said, touching upon a discussion they had while getting ready for bed. "When I told you that your cousin was a calculating bitch with impure motives – you gave me *a look*."

"I know your feelings are hurt," Alex said, "I've been listening to you brood for the last hour."

"I don't hear an apology, Mr. Alex the American."

"In the fullness of time, Monsieur Laurent, le Français. As you know, some of the best moments in my life have been apologies. I did not hurt your feelings on purpose; it was just a tiff. You were pouting because I was at least, partly right?"

Laurent swirled his fingers in Alex's chest hair and shrugged noncommittally. "Do you like the novels of *Thomas Hardy*?"

"I only really remember *Far from the Madding Crowd*. Why?"

"I could be Bathsheba Everdene."

"I love the old movie," Alex said, "with Julie Christie and Terence Stamp – he pried open Fanny's coffin and found the baby. Odd that you mention it. I remember thinking Terence Stamp made a heavenly Sergeant Troy. That scene with the flashing swords? That penis symbolism was something to behold."

"I was more obsessed with Julie Christie. If I ever do high camp, I'll be Julie Christie."

"You haven't got the right hair."

"I will get a wig."

"Think about the subject often, do you?" he smiled, scruffing up Laurent's hair."

"No. I think about *real* things," Laurent said sadly.

"There is no reality," Alex said gently, "that's the biggest illusion of all. Reality is something we conjured up, an attempt to give a fixed reference point to the chaos of existence. The thought of reality made us feel better, but in the end, they are only phantasms."

"Not always," Laurent said. "Maybe those phantasms are what life is all about?"

"Maybe," Alex agreed

"It's real that we're alive – and that we're all going to die. But death itself isn't real," he claimed, "it is something we only know about, we do not know it, we do not know what it is. I suspect there's a great deal more to dying than simply dying."

Confused but stimulated by the contradictory turmoil of his thoughts, Alex lifted Laurent's hand and gently kissed his fingers. "Go to sleep, Cinderella. You're turning into a pumpkin."

"You are afraid to think of death?" Laurent asked.

"I can't say for certain."

"The truth hurts?"

"No more or less than lies." Alex faced him, with an exceptional flash of emotion across his face. "I love our lives, Laurent."

Laurent waved his hand at the draperies he had chosen. "What's not to love?"

However, Alex was thinking about his dead Aunt Olivia now; he had tried so hard not to think about her over the last months. French nursery rhymes in the front seat of her car – his first strong memory of her, feeding him almond cookies in her kitchen, that always smelled like propane. He cherished those French nursery rhymes. Better even, the nights when she let him lie beside her in the hammock out by the pool – she often spent summer evenings with them – and she told him the story of the chocolate dog and the calico cat. Her voice had a quiet, self-absorbed fire, so much Olivia, and none other.

He doted upon her. She took him on long drives. When they stayed with oddball paternal relatives in Northern Maine Olivia entertained him, took him to an old cemetery, perched him upon headstones, and told him tales of pioneers until darkness fell. Another time, coming back to the house with her, they discovered a fire in a ceramic's factory, which the oddball relatives owned.

She used to phone him too early on Saturday mornings, never because she had anything important to say, only because she wanted to talk, or to recount a triviality. She was the only person Alex could think of who would phone him, wake him up, and yet keep him charmed. He never felt angry with her. Sometimes he felt she went too far, that she intruded, but he never felt upset. He would lie there on his back, covers tight up to his chin, and listen to her voice weave its magic. Olivia's voice sounded so beautiful on Saturday mornings, a snake-charming voice that whispered laughingly, promised him things, probed into his ideas.

Then she died of the same breast cancer that killed so many of the beautiful women in his family.

CHAPTER

5

Speeding down the country road toward their next French village, most of which were vastly less scenic than advertised – with MacDonald's restaurants and Starbucks, Byron slammed into a speed bump smack on. The rented Peugeot vaulted like a stunt car, landed on all fours, and off they roared. Charlotte had seen the speed bump in the road and knew Byron would hit it; thus, she pretended not to notice, though nonetheless she braced herself, continuing to work on her cuticles as he hit the bump and they leapt into the air, landing with a crunching wallop. She continued with her cuticle toiling, noticing in her peripheral vision that Byron stared at her. She pushed and buffed, as if utterly oblivious.

"Honeymoons are all the same," Byron said.

Charlotte, knowing he expected an answer, opted not to give one; she continued to concentrate with believable absorption on one of her cuticles. From her side vision, she noticed Byron stare at her again.

"Oh, for *Christ's sake*," Byron fumed.

"How did poor baby Jesus get involved in this fiasco?" Charlotte said, in what Byron referred to as her Spence voice. New York's finest prep schools had educated them both.

"All honeymoons have problems," he told her. "Roaches in Mexican hotels, diarrhea, lost luggage – "

"Hideous French villages with MacDonald's restaurants, leaded car exhaust, and miniature hotel rooms looking out on a Gap store and hookers?" With a pretend long look out the window at a field of melons. "Performance – *issues?*"

"Yes," Byron said. "Those too."

Taking a brief break from her nails, she reached over, took his favored guidebook, rolled down her window, and hurled it into the melon field."

"*What the heck*," he gasped.

"It lies like my Aunt Camilla."

He continued to stare at her; she returned to her nails.

"Look," he said, we agreed to see Paris, rent a car, do the French countryside, and then fly home via Nice. We've made all the reservations."

"Have we really? *Pity*," she said.

He could think of nothing to say; returning his eyes to the road.

After more minutes of purposeful torture, as she pretend-worked on a cuticle, she said, "Look – Byron – you're clearly as fed up as I am. That little James Bond routine back there was WASP for, 'This is a Holy-Mary-Mother-of-God-fucking-shit-miserable honeymoon.' So, may I suggest?"

He nodded his head without looking at her.

"Was that a yes nod or just a nervous twitch?"

"You sound like your father," he said.

"Hardly surprising since he *is* my father."

After a sigh, Byron said, "Yes, Charlotte, you may make a suggestion."

"The only guidebook I trust is this French one we bought in Paris," and she touched the cover. "It says that this Godiche village, where we are apparently staying tonight is – to my *enormous surprise* – the real thing: no MacDonald's and lovely untouched architecture. As I recall, we booked their largest room, overlooking the village square?"

"We did – *you did.*"

"Prescient of me, as it turns out. Anyway, tonight is their little summer carnival – the shortest night of the year fête. Who knows? Could be fun in a kind of France does Iowa. I suggest we bribe the hotel into letting us stay there for the rest of our honeymoon, in that spacious room with windows that do not look out on burger joints and hookers wearing chains. We can scamper on down to Nice next week and fly home."

Byron gave her a quick appraising look, returned his gaze to the road, and said, "What are the chances the room will be available for a week in the summer?"

"Because this is only village on our itinerary that is truly *nowhere* – so, who'd want to stay here, other than idiots like us? Besides, I'm Charlotte Fairfield; my people were born to cut deals. We might even hike tomorrow – or something rustic of that sort – I don't know, wander down country lanes, and steal juicy melons."

They were just passing Alex and Laurent's house and Charlotte pointed, "*Oh – my – God,* that's the prettiest house I've ever seen – I mean, like it beats anything in the Hamptons hands down."

Byron slowed to have a look, and then pulled over to the shoulder next to a stone wall. "It's amazing."

A pair of golden Labradors frisked beneath the ancient trees shading the restored stone façade of the house.

"Who do you suppose lives there?" Charlotte asked.

"The local aristocracy, I should imagine. It's not new money, that's certain."

At that precise moment, Sandrine (carrying her daily bag of stolen melons) walked by their car in her sandals and dirty blouse. She blew a puff of smoke in their direction as she mumbled, *"Va te faire foutre, trouducs."*

Byron looked at Charlotte in surprise. "That homeless woman just called us assholes and told us to fuck off."

"Yes. I heard. I'm like deeply offended," she said with mock emotion. She pointed out the window. "I want a house like that, Byron."

They both gazed longer.

"Let's hike back out tomorrow and have a proper look-see," Byron suggested. "It's beautiful out here, with the mixture of woodland and fields."

"So," she said, "We have a plan."

"Yes," he said, with a sense of weary relief, "we have a plan."

"Let's just be sure we take some notes, so that we know how to get back here."

Moreover – fortunately as it turned out – Byron, the high I.Q. mental wizard, did precisely that. He memorized the way back to Alex and Laurent's house.

Byron had always taken pride in mental prowess – the tall and handsome, class genius at his all boy's prep school. Well, *nerd* and genius, winner of every academic award offered at Collegiate School and graduating at the top of his class from Harvard. Early on, he discovered that people eroticized handsome geeks as much as the studly athletes.

So Byron reveled in his weirdly popular love for mathematics, poetry and his uncanny calculations of the odds on anything, as well as an aura of utter cleanliness with the aroma of old-fashioned soap, different colored socks, permanently perfect hair which even wind and rain couldn't damage, and a collection of bizarre patches from peculiar organizations in various languages For example, on the inside of his blazer he had attached a patch from a lesbian swimming league in Oslo, with a voluptuous mermaid beneath the words **Pupper og slag, kjæresten-pai**, as well as other esoteric behaviors common to the geek world.

Sex had never been important to Byron (at least two-people sex). He much preferred writing sonnets, villanelles, sestinas and pantoums, and the simple beauty of quadratic equations and a Star Trek marathon followed by good old-fashion masturbation made for a near-perfect Saturday night. His only two-person sex had been with his friend Martin on a weekend campout, which amounted to a bit of feeling up under the guise of measuring one another's erect manhood and then a contest to see who could shoot the farthest. Byron won by a good foot or more, but then it wasn't really the sort of accomplishment that even geeks talk about.

Charlotte, whom he first met on the train up to Boston from New York, when she commandeered seats for them with the no-nonsense attitude of a Storm Trooper, was the only woman he had ever dated – unless you called dates those evenings when he wrote essays and did the math homework for his downstairs neighbors who always contrived to make a display of their charms while he did their work for them. Without so much as a passionate kiss, Charlotte just took on the mantle of girlfriend, fiancée and now his wife.

Byron fiddled with the old-fashioned key in the lock, then pushed open the door and they stepped into an enormous room. It ran the width of the hotel, with a canopied bed at one end and a fireplace with settee and fauteuil at the other. Charlotte pointed at the planked oak floor and the antique table and chairs on which someone had put a vase with fresh flowers. Two sets of French windows looked out over the town square, with all its manic preparations for tonight's summer festival. Byron walked to one of the sets of doors and looked out with a whistle. When she joined him, Charlotte simply said, "*Wow*," in a hushed, wondrous voice.

"Well, Dorothy," he said, "we're not in Kansas anymore."

In the years in which they had dated, lived together, and finally honeymooned, neither Charlotte nor Byron had experienced intimacy as they did that day in Godiche. They flopped on their backs on the big bed and talked – sharing everything from stories of first and second grade, family reunions, opinions on which parts of New Jersey were habitable, ultimately agreeing only on certain portions of Bergen County. They laughed more than ever they had laughed. Charlotte found it hilarious that Byron ended up in the Headmaster's office daily at St. Bernard's for contradicting at least one of his teachers.

She particularly loved his sixth-grade story of how he had informed Miss Zehlik that, when she made an error in her own super-rigid St. Bernard's classroom rules and she said, "Well, I'm the teacher, I have the right to be exempted in my own classroom," Byron raised his hand and told her in his outraged sincerity, "*Miss Zehlik*. One *cannot* earn the right to do something wrong." Charlotte giggled over it for a good ten minutes. Fortunately, they chose their dinner destination at lunch, when they spotted a cute café on the village square and made reservations for 10:00 (or *22 heures)* as Byron said with an elegant fluency.

Now, Byron sat naked at the desk, sending an email to his mother, who couldn't – or more likely, *wouldn't* – do texts. Every time he spoke with with his mother – which was less and less often, despite the fact that they lived five blocks apart, one of those unmentioned blessings of life in New York – Byron felt the looming presence of her eternal and worsening domination. He looked up from his laptop and saw his face in the mirror. No one is as handsome at thirty-two as he was at twenty-two. That, Byron thought, is a Jane Austen-worthy universal truth.

He saw himself reflected in that mirror above the hotel desk, with his neatly coifed hair that had just the right amount of gel in it, hair that resumed its shape no matter the stress it endured, from hours of climbing the rocks in Central Park or hours standing at the seashore thinking. Still looking at himself in the mirror, Byron recalled that even as a child he never looked mussed. In summer, flies landed on his brother Teddy but not on him. In winter, his shoes never muddied. His bicycle remained as clean after ten years of use as the day his grandparents bought it for him. At school, his homework invariably came in the neatest. Byron exuded cleanliness. His maternal grandfather worked quality control on military planes, a difficult job; his personality owed to DNA encoding, Byron tended to think.

Byron's exceptional beauty, indigo eyes, and a fluffy oriole of hair, had always allowed him to wear clothes well. People ogled him in jeans and a tank top at the grocery store and at the opera in evening wear, even though Byron never made the slightest effort to look sensual. It just *happened*. Byron wore clothes well – Charlotte willing. She had recently exercised Valkyrian bossiness about his wardrobe. Raised one of two children of a civilized household on the Upper East side, he grew up in a townhouse approximately the size of Rhode Island within spitting distance of the trees in Central Park. He attended the best independent schools in Manhattan. Much about Byron's life bore tribute to civility: weekends in their house in the country, hours of volunteer work (usually without telling anyone, long before volunteer work organized by one's school became fashionable – and braggable).

Until ten years ago, he never gave tragedy a thought. Then, one afternoon, Byron turned on the television, transfixed as a reporter recounted a fire at a local station, a handsome news anchor seriously burned, in fact taken to the burn unit with burns over most of his body. A light had set something on fire and the something had fallen on Teddy, the news anchor, enveloping him in its burning dreadfulness. They even had ghastly images and photo-camera videos, of his burning brother stumbling around screaming. Teddy died – with everything played out in full view of the gruesome-loving public. Teddy's favorite Chopin etude accompanied his death – tanked to the gills on morphine.

Now, at the center of Byron's until now comfortable world lurked a thing both hard and hot: his only brother, his mother's undisguised – in fact openly admitted – favorite, had died in the grisliest public fashion. Byron felt Teddy's haunting memory always amongst them, lurking in shadows and closets, a morbid presence, a peculiar odor, the unvoiced death, the unacknowledged guest at dinners. Not that Byron ever voiced these uncharitable thoughts. Byron's nature excluded the public voicing of uncharitable thoughts.

"What are you doing?" Charlotte asked sleepily, rousing round from amid the deep and comfortable bed. Then, when their eyes met in the mirror, she sat up and said, "You're thinking about Teddy."

"Yes."

They stared at one another for a long while in the mirror, as Charlotte considered her next words. Finally, she said, "Byron, you know, a mother – well – I'm going to be one, I hope, and – okay, let me put it out there, if I ever have a son burnt to a crisp – well, I'll fucking rail at the world a damned sight more articulately than that idiot King Lear."

Charlotte speaking such a truthful statement startled Byron; again, they regarded one another. "They let him die," Byron said, "it's what the doctor *and* the Episcopal Chaplain thought was best. Not that he could have lived – the odds were – well –"

"Even more reason to look at it from your mom's point-of view. I mean, she knew what it meant, but she – well, she wanted him alive. I don't agree with her on that, but the mother is always – well, frankly, she's always right."

"No, she's not. That's an amazingly illogical statement. And in this case, my mother was being a selfish bitch, because they would have had to split open his skin like a frankfurter, remove his charred penis, and replace liters and liters of plasma and liquid – with him screaming as they did the debriding – scraping off the dead skin, which unfortunately is still connected to tender nerve endings. It was ..." and he choked up for a moment.

"He needed to go," Charlotte said, "I agree. It was right to let him die. Nevertheless, your mom sat there with tears running down her face. And even your dad fainted, right?"

"He thought it would help if he accompanied my mother to Teddy's last moments of – what? Basking in the Chopin Teddy couldn't even hear. However, he couldn't take it. My dad, the toughest damn, attorney on earth, fell over backward in a faint, caught at the last moment by an orderly or he'd be dead. Why did they choose morphine for Teddy? Why not intravenous *Tequila*? Tequila was always his fave."

"Byron – I mean, can you *imagine* how freaking hard must that be on a mother? Fucking hell, my heart has always gone out to your mom. She's a heroine in my eyes and always will be. No surprise she's wonder woman. She's had to be, hasn't she?"

Byron's mother, who'd been staying with her Airedale terriers in their vast country house, came to visit Byron two months ago, an unannounced and unsuccessful trip.

"She demands too much of you," she told Byron over a glass of wine on the veranda of Byron's penthouse. Balustrades curved round them like the stage-set of an Italian villa.

The visit coincided, unfortunately, with a time when Byron wasn't sure just where he fit into the world in which he lived. Although a diligent worker, he always had projects, like painting the den or redecorating one of the upstairs guestrooms, and he always enjoyed them. He did their shopping, from groceries to clothes, gassed the car, kept it washed, took their shirts and pants to the cleaner. He was as much one part of the relationship as he was the other – and it confused him that he liked the domestic parts best.

He learned to cook, and he cooked well. Nevertheless, Charlotte insisted on hiring a cleaning

lady, who came now two days a week, and so Charlotte never vacuumed, dusted, or washed a window.
Their friends came to visit from time to time. People always stayed with them in their to-die-for-
penthouse, and there were invariably dinner
parties they hosted for visiting writers or actors, or
others who come to New York.

"Charlotte loves me, mom, and I love her."

"*And the sex?*"

Byron flushed scarlet; he said nothing.

"No surprises there. *Ha.* You went shopping
in the wrong market for a life mate, Byron."

"*Mother,*" Byron said.

"You did, Sunshine, and you'll realize it in
your time and way. And this isn't a life," she waved
her hand out over the weathered balustrade toward
the panorama of city below them.

"Yes, mother. It is. This is the life for which
you raised me."

She looked at him. "You can seriously tell me
you're happy?"

"I said this is the life for which you raised
me. How does happiness enter into it?" Byron
stood up, went to the rail. "I know Charlotte seems
like a bully, but she's not – really."

"*Children?*"

"I don't know."

"Have you talked about it?"

He turned to her, back leaning against the
balustrade. Imagery occasionally haunted Byron:
paintings, photos, film stills, paintings. A woman

in an awkwardly elegant pose dominated the town-house in which Byron grew up. Grandmother – father's side, of course – sat on a chaise with a bulldog half in and half out of her lap. She wore a curiously long mink stole. She looked beautiful and ghastly, a waxen-faced socialite flaunting wealth. His mother embodied that portrait – the thought came to Byron in an Epiphany that afternoon.

"We haven't talked about it yet, mother – we're not even married."

"My son the almost-Asperger's child."

"Not a child anymore."

"My point remains."

Charlotte got up out of bed in her anorexic nudity and came to put her arms around his neck.

"Above anything else," she said, "you are and will always be my bestest friend."

"So – maybe we don't need children?"

She kissed the top of his head. "Maybe not, but if we can get things working – well, you'd be a good daddy."

"There's always adoption," he said, in his masterfully poor timing.

"Indeed. There are also gypsies you can pay to steal blond kids for you in Eastern Europe – cut-rate deals, I hear."

"Oh, God, that's not – I mean – *you know* I'll see a doctor – I'll – well ..." He kissed her forehead. "Swear."

"Silly. Stop now." Then, "Byron, do you believe in God? I mean, right, I know we're both Episcopalians and all that shit. But I mean, *really*, cards on the table – do you?"

He thought about it for what seemed a long while, drawing her closer against him. "I don't know. Probably not, though it feels strange to say that. God is illogical and – well, most belief-systems, ours included, are peasant-worthy ignorance. I do enjoy all of the ritual and, mysteriously, I find the liturgy quite tender."

"Tender?"

"Yes. Emotive. Affecting."

As was often the case, it took her a moment or two to digest his meaning, and then she told him, "I haven't believed in God for years – since I was like, I don't know, thirteen or something. But," and she gave his forehead a kiss. "This afternoon, I do believe in God – and here he is – in this amazing village."

"An unknown hamlet is where this all-powerful supernatural being chooses to live?"

"Good choice if you ask me," She said, then catching something on his face. "*What?* So, God should choose to live in Cleveland? Please. Byron –

you are *so Byron*. You always will be. They tossed away the mold when they made you. Anyway – this is where God is, because," and she gestured out the *porte-fenêtre*, "it is real and beautiful and filled with kind people."

He smiled. "I suspect the ratio of kind to vile is the same here as anywhere."

"Without knowing it, darling, you are more or less quoting Bruce Springsteen."

He burst out laughing. "Good grief. *Is he still alive?*"

"He is – and tight with that fat-ass former New Jersey thug Governor."

Again, he laughed. "And you are Charlotte, and you will *always* be Charlotte."

Lizzy made an angry snort at Alex's remark about her seeming different. "I'm wearing your father's goddamned Australian hunting crap, which is as cheap as Walmart sells as far as I can tell – and I very much doubt he's wearing my sundresses and blouses."

Alex gave a stupefied glance at Laurent who returned the look.

"I meant – well, you seem *different*. I didn't mean your clothes."

"Where's Aunt Kitty? Can't she even be bothered to come greet me? *Fucking typical.*"

Another long silence filled with that lovely French countryside birdsong.

"I'm just going to say it, Lizzy. She's dead."

"*What?*"

"Dead."

"She died *here*?" and she pointed at their house.

"Actually, just about exactly where you're standing; we had it steam cleaned. It was one of those freak accidents. She'd just arrived, was gabbling about something, then grabbed one of her breasts, made this weird shrieking noise and dropped dead," he pointed to the spot.

He couldn't continue, because Lizzy had burst out laughing, which caused Sandrine to drop her bag of melons and laugh as well. The two women stood holding hands and guffawing, tears running down Lizzy's face – though clearly not tears of grief. Meanwhile, Dalton, mystified and frightened by the peculiarities of girls, had gone over to stand next to Laurent and Alex.

"We salvaged – that's a word?" Laurent asked.

"Yes," Dalton told him.

"Thank you. Her wig. It's in the kitchen."

Lizzy only laughed harder, finally turning to the men and saying in French, forgetting about Dalton's linguistic limitations, "I'm sorry. I know she was your mother, Alex, and of course, I'm sorry for you – to lose your mother, I mean. But Jesus fucking Christ I hated that mean-spirited, back-biting, cheap-ass *bitch*."

Laurent made the French gesture for enough-already and was about to say something, but Lizzy stopped him short. She made a forgive-me face at Alex, saying "I shouldn't talk that way about your mother, Alex, and I apologize, but she treated me like *monkey shit* my whole life – and the idea of her keeling over from a heart attack right on your doorstep –," but bursting into wild, cackling laughter again she couldn't continue.

Sandrine gave Lizzy another kiss and said again to Alex and Laurent. "I am fucking *loving* this woman."

Alex tried to herd everyone into the house, but no one cooperated. Sandrine and Lizzy were engaged in a deep philosophical discussion about the general hellishness of life. He overheard Lizzy rattle off in French, "Sometimes I think I've gained greater clarity, and then I realize it's just another fucking goddamned illusion – because that's what life's been for me, a shitty string of illusions."

Meanwhile, Laurent – for whom flirting represented one of his cultural inheritances – regaled a visibly bored Dalton with descriptions of various trees and flowers, the whole time testing out the strength of Dalton's bicep and touching the various contours of his hairy chest, none of which phased Dalton in the least, although he looked as if he might topple over in a faint. He had clearly passed beyond exhaustion into another universe entirely.

Finally, using a combination of Australian sheep dog techniques, whistles and flapping arms, Alex got them through the door of the mudroom and into the kitchen. At her first sight of Kitty-Louise's wig, Lizzy burst out in giggles, provoking her comrade Sandrine to put the wig on her head and dance around the kitchen, to the accompaniment of Lizzy's increasingly hysterical laughter.

Alex kept mumbling, "*Hello*, respect for my dead mother? *Hello?*"

Dalton accepted a glass of mineral water from Laurent and downed it in one long gulp, holding it out for more.

When their eyes met, Alex asked Dalton, "She really has no luggage?"

He shrugged, "It was all your dad's hunting stuff, so she just abandoned it on the train."

Lizzy took a break from laughing to say, "*Cheap ass* polyester crap."

Alex, undone by it all – his mother's death, Lizzy's bizarre transmogrification, Sandrine, Laurent as vamp – simply fell on a chair and put his head into his hands.

Things had calmed down, and Alex corralled Lizzy in one of the downstairs sitting rooms. While Alex threw himself into one of the overstuffed fauteuils, Lizzy paced the room, at last coming to rest at one of the *porte-fenêtres* looking out on the immensity of their tree-filled property.

"So," Alex said.

"So," Lizzy said back.

Alex's intended conversation flat-lined. He listened to one of Laurent's expensive antique clocks – he preferred the Louis-Philippe style, though Alex had yet to decipher the subtleties of that style, since Louis Philippe clocks looked like the clocks made on either side of the so-called citizen King. Watching Lizzy stand morosely at the window in his father's clothes made him feel as if the last few days had come to their inevitable breaking point. He started to cry, but silently, his tears spilling out faster than he could wipe them away.

Intuition caused Lizzy to turn around and look at him. "I'm sorry about Aunt Kitty-Louise," she said.

"No, you're not."

She stared at him with an intense expression.

"I don't give a rat's ass about my mom dying," Alex said, "the homophobic bitch."

"Bitch or not – which she was, sure as I'm standing here – everyone feels it when their mother dies. You're an orphan once your mom's gone, no matter how nasty she was."

"It is bizarre to say that I watched her die." He thought about that. "Actually, she was already dead by the time I noticed her. I only turned around because she stopped talking – she was right in the middle of criticizing something about the house – and Laurent screamed. He doesn't manage crises well, but fortunately Sandrine turned up soon after."

Lizzy nodded, still with an intensely wordless – *something*.

"Did you know she wore a wig?" Alex asked.

"*Know*? I fucking picked it out. She shanghaied me one Saturday morning and forced me to drive her all the way down through fucking snowdrifts and past State Trooper check points to *goddamned Des Moines* with her, so that no one in Sioux City would find out."

"*I* never knew."

Lizzy shrugged. "I think it's just another example of getting what you pay for. That thing cost a shitload. It isn't cheap buying the hair off the head of a poor Bolivian woman."

"Lizzy, what's with all the swearing, and – *what*? Negativity, I guess."

She turned quickly away and stared again out the window.

"Lizzy?"

Nothing.

"*Liz*?"

"What?" she said, hard toned, without turning around.

"What *what*? I asked you a question."

"I'm not really sure you did, Alex."

"*Huh*?"

She stood silently.

"Do I even know you?" Alex asked. "

She offered him a continuing view of her back.

He remained silent, settling back into the chair. Again, the clock ticked maddeningly. Water ran somewhere. Far off pipes gurgled.

"*Fuck you*," Lizzy said, abruptly breaking the silence.

"*What?* Fuck *you*, guest o'mine."

"Oh, yeah, right – guest. What shit," Lizzy said. "Tell me you haven't been dreading my visit for months. You know damn well what my I.Q. is, so you think I don't know why Sandrine is here? *Screw you, Alex* – at best you've only ever tolerated me, which I knew the whole time. I was just putting on that jabber-jaw happy-go-lucky bullshit. You know how come I never had any money? It wasn't because I spent it on – fuck it, whatever Aunt Kitty-Louise used to call it, fripperies or some-thing." Then she rounded on him, glaring with a long-repressed fury. "It was because I was paying to see an honest-to-God psychiatrist to give me drugs and keep me from killing myself; I was so shit mis-erably unhappy."

"*You were?* What I remember is that you were always hanging around me laughing and car-rying on. Hell, I remember you admiring my morn-ing erection once."

"I recall the morning. Your mother sent me in to wake you up. The erection comment was merely a courtesy upgrade for being a relative," she snapped.

He could think of nothing to say; he said nothing.

Lizzy continued to glare at him.

In the end, Alex stood up and – stunning himself with his own pent-up vehemence – said, "So you're a fucking fake. Congratulations on carrying it off. You were an irritating piece of shit, coming into my bedroom uninvited, talking about crap, inviting yourself to my parties, and – *yeah* – I hated that. Frankly, I have absolutely no idea how I really feel about you – except that at this moment I think you're as manipulative a bitch as my mother. I hope your shrink *has* helped you because you sure as hell need it." He shook a finger at her, and he watched it tremble, so angry had he become. "You practically *ruined* my high school years, hanging around me like some goofy nerd with dyed hair and Goth outfits. Anyway, I'll see you in the morning, asshole – an asshole whom I *did* tolerate, you're right about that, when I didn't have to, did I?"

She merely shrugged at him.

"So – some credit? Another courtesy upgrade? Tolerating you had to be some kind of love, that's for damn sure, because like everyone else in Sioux City I *always* thought you were off your rocker – which, it would now appear, you were."

She unrelentingly stared at him, then made a spitting sound, touching her fingers to an imaginary radiator and made a sizzle noise. "Feel better?"

"Oh, for the love of – whatever."

"Usually, God, but what they hey – let's say 'for the love of Princess Diana. Wasn't she a gay icon?"

They glared at one another.

"I wrote a poem once about how you treated me,' she said, "it was published, in fact – though not in any of those magazines with half naked men in thongs and handcuffs so I doubt either you or Laurent read it."

A long, far too long, pause snuffed out the room's air.

"How I treated *you?*"

"I was having some frozen yogurt at the mall, when you and all your friends traipsed by my table. You saw me – we both know you saw me. I had a mouth full of Butter Pecan yogurt, so I *couldn't* say anything. But I thought *you* would. You didn't. Pretending not to see me, which was one big *unfunny* joke, you and your gang just walked away. I stayed with my yogurt, which was melting anyway. It's titled "My Cousin Having Ignored Me."

To be ignored is cruel
Irony, which plays
Insecurity
Against itself in a
Destructive duel of
Desire. And no
Retaliation,
Since you must exist

To seek your revenge,
And denial is
Vengeless cold longing.

With steely uncaring and thinking the poem nothing more than an exercise in self-pity – he said, "Laurent's giving out the keys and room assignments – so go fucking find him." On that, Alex turned and walked out of the room.

Until she opened the door on a dripping wet, naked, hairy chested Dalton did it occur to Lizzy that Alex and Laurent would assume that she and Dalton were a couple.

"Hi," he said, in that breezy boy way, continuing to towel his head.

"Shit," she said. "They've put us in the same room.

"*Rooms*," he told her, belatedly wrapping the towel around his waist. "There's like this enormous living room, library thing through there," and he pointed, "A bathroom like from fucking Versailles with a shower I didn't even know existed in Europe." Then it dawned on him. "Oh, fuck, Lizzy, don't make me move," he pleaded, gesturing toward the bed, "We can share – really – look at it, it's like a real American queen size."

Lizzy looked a while at the bed, set into a hunter green alcove near French windows that opened on flower boxes filled with multi-colored blossoms.

"You can practice up on your blow-job skills," then seeing that was the wrong direction, he hurriedly added, "Joke, *joke, Lizzy.* I mean, for real we can both fit in that big bed, no problem. I won't hog more than my side, promise," and he held his hands up in a way meant to be reassuring, but it made his towel fall off, once again revealing his huge penis and quite beautiful testicles.

"Whatever," Lizzy said, tossing her borrowed bag of feminine articles from Sandrine, holding things like a gigantic bra and panties tight enough to squeeze Barbie, in the direction of the bathroom.

"So," he reiterated in that irksome way of boys, who never got subtlety, unless they were gay. It ought to be the litmus test, she thought. "You're cool with sharing?"

She pointed to the bathroom. "I'm taking the fucking longest shower in the history of showers, and afterward I intend to sleep in that bed for about twelve generations. You're welcome to sleep on the right side," then remembering how stupid boys so often were about things like this she pointed, "There – *that side.*"

Laurent and Alex lay on their backs in bed, holding hands as they always did before sleeping. They'd been silent for half an hour when Alex said, "You were certainly playing the flirt with Dalton."

"Pooh – it was half an effort. Anyway, he's stupid."

"I doubt that."

"Why?"

"Something in his face. I'd say there's more to Dalton than meets the eye, and he's about as straight as they come, that's for sure."

"American straight – which I find, well – you know."

"Yes." In their home, they had long discussed the differences between Americans and French-men. Then Alex said, "Laurent, I don't think I've ever been so unhappy."

After a pensive moment, Laurent said. "I dis-agree. That is nonsense."

"Okay – put it this way: I'm not happy."

"Why *should* you be happy?" Laurent asked.

"I don't think I *should* be I'm just saying that I'm not."

"Because of that Lizzy creature in drag."

Despite himself, Alex smiled, remembering one of their favorite songs, "Andrew in Drag," by the Magnetic Fields. "I don't know."

"*Normal*," Laurent said, in the French fashion, pronouncing it as nor*mal*."

"But what's happened to her? She's changed into this – this – *gorgon*. She's mean and bitter and full of nastiness."

"I think, with time," Laurent said, in his philosophical voice, "you will find that you are wrong about that. She's not a gorgon. However, she has emerged – at last."

"*Emerged?*"

"From her Chrysalis, like a butterfly."

They were speaking in French now, having switched with Laurent's nor*mal*. Alex said something translatable into English as, "Nothing makes any sense."

"Normal."

"Not for me it isn't."

"*Pooh*," Laurent said, "you and that American desire to have everything be linear sequential. Life isn't meant to make sense. People get diseases, earthquakes and Tsunamis destroy cities and even countries. Where is the sense in that? Love makes sense, and that's all that matters, Alex," and Laurent gave Alex's hand a loving squeeze and leaned over to kiss him.

"Okay, then – for me it seems as if everything I knew has been turned on its head."

"You are troubled by more than your mother's bizarre death at our front door? Though, for me, it felt right that she dies there. She hated the two us being together and she hated our house.

So, the house took its vengeance, out of love for us. I will always cherish the house for killing your horrible mother, and I hope that we never move from here – *ever*."

A long silence full of birdsong. Then Alex said softly, "I love you, Laurent."

"And I love you, *mon chouchou*. "I always knew that we were missing something important about Lizzy. I should have been smart enough to see it," Alex said.

"You were; you did."

"If I did, then it was subliminal."

"We create others as we wish them to be," Laurent said. "It's --"

"Yes," Alex agreed. "Nor*mal, mon inséparable chérie* – "

Silence and another squeeze of Alex's hand served as Laurent's answer that he understood.

"Poor Lizzy," Alex said.

"Why poor Lizzy?"

"To be so unhappy that she felt suicidal – to be so misunderstood."

"She was understood as she wished to be understood," Laurent said.

"Do you think we should have told them about the festival?"

"No, No, no. My mother said something about village idiots prancing in clogs – and I hardly think either Lizzy or Dalton is in the mood for dancing."

"I love you, Laurent."

"But of course. You are a smart man."

And with a kiss, Alex rolled over, curled Laurent up in his arms, and they both prepared to sleep.

The Godiche Summer Festival – *L'Estivale Godiche* – had rooted itself so deeply in the loamy soil of the Vendée that it predated the first Ice Age. Chiefly it consisted of staying up all night between the shortest sunset / sunrise of the year, getting competitively drunk, and singing strange folk songs to which no one really knew the words (though they pretended with drunken enthusiasm). However, the organizers also held games, some of which confirmed the Festival's Druidic origins – such as hurling long knives at demon-painted melons and a tug-of-war between one man and one draught horse. The horse always won, obviously, so the contest winner proved the one most capable of being dragged face down the longest distance without complaining – or, as happened at least once each year, forcing the Mayor to summon an ambulance from the hospital in Fontenay-le-Comte.

The highlight of the festival was the dance competition, in which registered teams – who had been practicing all year – performed historic Vendean dances, clad in all of the frills, leather and paraphernalia of some long-forgotten era.

Byron and Charlotte had been savoring their meal and were finishing off their espresso. "Why?" Byron asked.

She arched her brows.

"Oh. Right," he said. "I promised to listen."

A bird whistled plaintively on the church eaves. They watched it for several minutes.

"Well?" Byron said.

"I don't know where to start."

"The beginning?"

"There is no beginning," she said.

"Something with no beginning sounds worrying. Does it have an end?"

She looked perturbed.

"Just say what's on your mind, Charlotte."

She held her hair back from her face and peered at him. "I think you're gay, Byron."

He flushed. Quiet moments filled up with bird song; neither spoke, nor did they look at each other.

Then Charlotte said, "I don't think it's terrible or anything, I think it's fine, I do. But that's what I think's troubling you, that's why I think you're unhappy."

He still said nothing.

"Byron?"

He looked out the window at the rivers of moss on the bricks, at how an oak tree filled up the space between the sacristy and the sky. What could he say to this? 'You've hit the nail on the head there, Charlotte, my love.' 'I fancy men all right, Charlotte, good on.' His emotions quivered. Torn equally between confession and rejection, he wished himself far away, another planet. He wished himself to the very ends of the earth, where water thundered in cataracts off the edge of the known world and sea serpents played and no one could find him, know him, or reach out to him. He wanted oblivion and life at the same time. Nevertheless, this was Charlotte sitting next to him, his wife, so rejection was no easier than confession. Wishing himself far away was a ridiculous impossibility, so he let the creeping paralysis hold him. He gave voice to no thoughts. Then, "*Oh, hell* – I've left my wallet in the room."

"How convenient."

"I'm serious. It's still in the room."

"I'm sure they'd let us come back and pay to-morrow."

"No, No," Byron said, "that's not right." He glanced at his watch. "Look, you sit here, and bask in the good wine, and I shall gallantly go and re-trieve said wallet from our room."

"Okay," she said sleepily, lifting her face up with a smile of gratitude.

Byron explained the situation to the owner, who shrugged his reluctant Gallic acceptance, and then Byron was out the door, sprinting toward their hotel. Off in the distance, on the horizon, he saw something glowing and growing bright, which he found extremely peculiar – but then he was in the hotel lobby, where he paused for a fateful moment to speak with Madame the owner. Then, he turned away from her and made it to the bottom of the stairs when – well, he could never, even years later find the words to explain what happened.

In essence, Byron came to, as one does from a faint, inside what was left of the brick storeroom at the bottom of the staircase, naked except for his boxers – though they were around his ankles. The rest of the hotel seemed to have disappeared with his clothes, though he could feel the heat from fire on all sides. He stood up, nearly passed out, steadied himself on the brick wall and tried to gain his bearings. What was left of Madame the owner, was impaled on the sign of the building next door – visible because the lobby of the hotel had disappeared, replaced by human body parts, and bits of metal, and other things his mind would never recall, despite many years of therapy.

Once he came to enough to realize who and where he was, he thought at once of Charlotte. Since there was no front left to the hotel – clearly, he had survived only because of the use of iron rods in the brickwork of the hotel's 1950s storage room and vault and the fact that he was so thin. Had he been a centimeter wider the opening into the safety of the brick vault would have prevented him pulling through – he began to think more clearly and looked across the street to what was left of the restaurant.

What he saw was the cockpit of a gigantic plane burning where their table had been. An engine still operating at full throttle in the middle of the road, proceeding by dint of size and power to suck everything into it as Byron watched –until something finally caused it to explode in a massive boom of metallic detritus. Something hot and painful imbedded itself in Byron's leg.

He tried running toward the remains of the restaurant but found that it was virtually impossible with bare feet. Looking around he saw two separate legs – fortuitously both male – and without caring a hoot for propriety and not feeling the least bit squeamish (a first for Byron) he pulled a size 10 off one leg – too small by a longshot, but it would have to do, into which he crammed his foot, amid the other man's blood – and a roomier size 11 ½ from another man's leg, into which he stuffed his other foot. Then he was indeed able to run across the debris, human and otherwise, to the cockpit that had been a restaurant.

"*Charlotte*," he screamed. "*Charlotte.*"

But it was hopeless, and he turned away. Charlotte had gone. So he turned his attention to the street to see in what conceivable way a tall, thin man, clad in nothing more than mismatched shoes and Brooks Brother's boxers, could help.

Dalton leapt from bed and stormed over to the chair by the window. He had been trying to sleep as Lizzie thrashed and talked in her sleep and even seemed to be fighting someone, her fists punching the air. Rather than wake her, however, he chose to sit by the window.

A good decision, as it turned out, because he found himself thinking profoundly, as he looked off into the sinking mauve-orange greenish sunset. Dalton had done his best over the years to evade thinking. He had kept himself busy doing everything possible in High School and College: sports, music, plays, community service, extra classes – in which he always achieved an 'A', so that his advisor could not (in good conscience) stop him from taking even more.

Thus, Dalton had almost succeeded in avoiding thinking about – well, the things about which he did not wish to think. Here, however, jetlagged and sad, looking at the vivid hued melon fields and woodlands, he succumbed to the idea of contemplation – and he thought about himself, his future, his hopes, in a rush of awareness. For the first time in his life – or so it seemed – he wasn't anxious. How weird was that, he thought? In fact, he felt – what? *Peaceful?* Something of that sort.

The summer Dalton turned five – two days after, to be exact – his world changed for all time. His brother died of meningitis. It was a wide-pathed tornado of family tragedy: his mother's departure to a psychiatric facility, his grandmother's feeble but heavy-handed endeavor (for three months) to be Dalton's mother figure, his father's drinking and tears (make that sobs), Dalton's own bewilderment over how James went from having the flu – the doctor came to their house and diagnosed it – to being buried in a green and shady place where everyone wept while touching the top of Dalton's mystified head.

For weeks, Dalton – who had not understood the funeral – stood nightly at the open kitchen door and called out his brother's name, trying to sound like his mother when she called them home for dinner. James was merely lost. Where had that blaring truck with the spinning red lights taken him? Why didn't he come home? Where was Mama? It so entirely traumatized him that even now, in his sleep or when drunk, Dalton still called out for his brother to come home. James never did; and neither did that lost part of Dalton's soul.

In many ways, Dalton was as lost as James; he was a young man with a bright, brawny and beautiful body – but lacking its soul – an athletic champion earning straight A's who, as expected, chose an equally soulless creature for a girlfriend; someone who could never fill his abyss. Because his Kindergarten friends had moved away from Sioux City, as people tended to do, and others forgot about James, Dalton never spoke of his heartbreak. To speak of James would throw open locked doors and lift fastened windows. So, James lingered forever in limbo, together with Dalton's soul, both incapable of going home.

Dalton continued to play the role of a bright, beautiful, and brawny body, when he was really a man betrayed by a Godless world that stole away the lives of little children.

It might have been Kandy's idea to come to France, but Dalton was beginning to think that he would be the one who gained the most. Again, he raised his face and looked out over the spreading Vendée – and he pondered what he wanted to do next, and he felt so excited by it that his erection popped up above his boxers. Always a good sign, he thought, going back to bed.

CHAPTER

9

Lizzy had slept deeply but now lay awake, in that irritating electrical-jolting way of jetlag, listening to Dalton snore. He was, as she correctly guessed, a bed hog, sprawling all over the mattress. She thought about her strange transformation – or, more correctly, her honest stepping into the light. She felt unburdened – much more than running naked in Sioux City – even as she realized that she'd devastated Alex. Being French, Laurent took things like a complete change of personality in stride. Lizzy admired that. Of course, she did not intend to pursue cursing as a hobby; the cursing owed only to the freshness of her self-discovery after all those expensive years of pretending to optimism and happiness.

She let them go; she knew she'd never look back. Her psychiatrist had spent years telling her to do this, to let go – as well as giving her increasing dosages of Clonazepam, Wellbutrin, Lexapro, Paxil, Temazepam, and Xanax. She would never see the drug-pushing quack again and she intended to stop taking her drugs in the approved slow fashion about which she had read – though she rather liked her status as prescription drug addict.

She felt in with the in crowd. She'd heard that Clonazepam withdrawal was the worst, and occasionally caused fatal seizures – so, obviously, that attracted her curiosity. She reflected a while about not giving a damn about Aunt Kitty-Louise, but she worried more – at least for the moment – about her unsuccessful attempts to recall the words to the final stanza of Coleridge's "Khubla Khan." That was why she had awakened. She could only get,

"A damsel with a dulcimer
in a vision once I saw:
It was an Abyssinian maid,
and on her dulcimer she played."

It exasperated her that in her angry jet-lag fugue she could not remember her favorite poem. She gave bed hog Dalton a swift kick.

He opened his eyes, looked at her, and said, "What the fuck?"

"Oh, for Christ's sake don't start with me, Dalton, you've been kicking me and stealing the duvet for an hour."

"It's too hot for a duvet and, in fact, it's called a couette in France. Look," and he pointed at the windows. "It's still light out."

"Yes, it's called the summer solstice. The longest day of the year and all that?"

"I know what the solstice is, Lizzy, Geez." He stared at the lovely night sky. "Kandy and I were going to trek the world."

"Trek the world?" Lizzy huffed. "With what? A big sign that said, "Rich First-World White People Here to Ogle You Pitiful Creatures? I *detest* that kind of trek-the-world tourism."

"*Huh?*"

"Dalton, do you think tourism helps anyone but capitalists? It destroys our globe, from reefs to mountains to beaches. And what? You get to stamp away on Machu Pichu and get an iPhone full of digital images of peasant women in those god-awful British banker bowler hats – and the starving millions around the globe get – *what*? A meaningless tote-and-fetch tourist-related job.

He lay silent, thinking.

"Trek the world," she scathed again. "What privileged first world shit. You don't hear about many Rwandans trekking around the world unless they're trying to get to Europe as migrants."

He continued ruminating. Lizzy had clearly struck a nerve. Finally, he said, "It was Kandy's idea."

"What the Hell does it matter whose idea it was? It's wrong, whoever produced it."

Another long silence.

"*Hello?*" she said.

"What do you want from me?" he said brusquely.

"I only wanted to know if you were awake."

"No, I'm sleeping soundly, can't you tell?"

"I was reared on that passive-aggressive Sioux City tone, so it's wasted on me," she said.

"If I'm not snoring, I'm awake. Okay?"

"Why did you bark at me like that?" she said. "That was a bit harsh."

"Because you woke me up, apparently to ask me if I was awake, and I'm tired as Hell and jet-lagged and you deserved barking at because now you're acting like a pretentious asshole."

"Wow. You ever get this snarky with Kandy? Because I'd wager big money that you never would have dared."

He shrugged. "Why'd you kick me? To find out if I was awake?" he asked, having decided he wasn't talking about Kandy anymore. In truth, he was glad Kandy was gone and he was free to – well, he was working that part out.

"Because I harbored the idiotic idea that you might just know the final stanza to Coleridge's 'Khubla Khan.' You were an English major if I remember correctly."

After a jaw-wrenching yawn, he said sleepily:

"A damsel with a dulcimer In a vision once I saw: It was an Abyssinian maid, And on her dulcimer she played, Singing of Mount Abora. Could I revive within me Her symphony and song, To such deep delight 'twould win me That with music loud and long, I would build that dome within the air! That sunny dome, those caves of ice, And all who heard should see them there, And all should cry: "Beware! Beware! His flashing eyes, his floating hair! Weave a circle 'round him thrice,

And close your eyes in holy dread:
For he on honeydew hath fed,
And drunk the milk of Paradise!"

"Excellent. Thanks," She said, running over the words in her mind.

"*That's all?*"

"That's all – what?" She asked.

"I fucking recite a stanza from memory of the sexiest semen exploding from a penis poem in history – and no, '*Wow*,'" no, 'My God, Dalton, you are such an intellectual stud."

"Dalton," she sighed, "You're so Sioux City."

"Jesus, you're cruel these days. I can't fucking help where I was born and raised. You think I wouldn't rather have been born and raised in – where? San Francisco or New York?"

She thought about that, and the strange way in which he said it. Once again, she had the sense that Dalton had a deeper and more mysterious – *something* than any of them had given him credit.

"Why are you trying to remember Coleridge, anyway?" he asked.

She started to cry.

"*Lizzy?*"

"Sorry. Go back to sleep."

"But –?"

"It's just the combination of my fucked up, lonely life and jetlag – and I'm not Kandy, I don't need to be cuddled and fucked when I'm sad."

He gave a tired, bitter yelp of a laugh.

"What's so funny?"

"I vowed not to talk about her anymore, but the very idea of Kandy wanting to be fucked. She hated sex, which was pretty much okay by me."

"*Really?*"

"Really. Just because she had big boobs and that Sioux City whore look didn't mean she was – in fact, she was as frigid as an iceberg."

"Sounds terrible."

"What's that old saying? We are the choices we make?"

They looked at each other.

"Okay," Lizzie said.

"Okay," he said back.

"It sounds trite, but my God, you can do so much better than Kandy Hawthorne," Lizzy told him. "I mean – *hello?* Have you had a good look at yourself? And, yes, it is impressive that a hunk like you can recite Coleridge. Jesus, dreamy romantics love that stuff, you dummy. And a dreamy romantic is precisely what you need. Someone you will love you for both your body and your mind – which is a damned fine mind, Dalton."

"Thanks, Lizzy."

"It's the truth, so go back to sleep, and tomorrow we'll start scouting out some dreamy French romantic who also knows poems and likes to be fucked."

"We'll see," he said with a sleepy laugh. Then he rolled over and promptly went back to sleep.

Lizzy, on the other hand, lay there crying and – as it slowly grew dark outside – mentally composed the first draft of her "Sonnet of Sioux City Lizzy:"

Beautiful Lizzy
Lived her hidden hell
Prisoned in her cell
That made her crazy
As a raccoon, or
So Sioux said –
Where nose is not nez,
She searched French doors.
This made Lizzy poor
In Sioux City Lore.

A fully loaded Airbus 380 carries tons of fuel, luggage, freight, food, drinks, carts, pets, all manner of assorted plane detritus and about 500 passengers and crew. It has Rolls-Royce engines, which when fully throttled have a tornadic suction such as only found in a Sci-fi Star Wars tractor beam, and a deafening mechanical caterwauling that could easily compete with twenty Hoover Dams.

In fact, unearthly roaring and *Wizard of Oz* suction offered the first inkling to the Godiche *L'Estivale* competition dancers and the packed audience in the village square of something Apocalyptic – well, that and the lights and flaming baleen carcass of an A380 as it appeared from the north. When it exploded, at around 1,000 feet, experts later explained that it would have resembled a mini-Hiroshima, including a mushroom cloud seen – and documented – as far away as Geneva, Switzerland.

Since Sunshine Air flight 666 exploded directly over Alex and Laurent's house, the Hiroshima effect – as they later learned –comparatively speaking, alone in Godiche, spared their house from destruction. Well, excluding the suctioned removal of their beloved stork's nest (stork and her eggs too, of course) from the chimney, the breaking of nearly every window, assorted bits and pieces tossed inside the house, and the gift of a half-naked first-class flight attendant, whose strapped in body and sturdy seat had embedded themselves in the south wall of the house.

Everything lower than her blouse accounted for the half-naked part – no panties, shoes, stockings – all of it unfortunately enhanced by the fact that her legs straddled the arms of the chair, clearly displaying her bikini-waxed crotch. Her coiffed hair and Sunshine Air chapeau burned for about half an hour before the fire mysteriously self-extinguished at her scalp, to the amazement of observers, who were uninitiated in the vicissitudes of burning bodies.

Lizzy had only just fallen back asleep when the house shook as if in an earthquake and she and Dalton sat upright to ear-splitting noise, an explosion and a bright fiery mass of light that covered the skyline. For several moments they sat there in bed, then they looked at one another, and

Dalton – white faced – pointed at a burning human corpse that had materialized in the armchair drawn closer to the window by the initial suction; the burning thing draped in a kind of seductive Garbo-esque pose.

Amid the glass were identifiable hands, feet, and one strangely undamaged head of an older woman with a look of complete surprise – sitting now on top of one of Laurent's Louis-Philippe clocks. A Longchamps suitcase had popped open on the floor beside the bed – and instinct correctly told Lizzy that she stared into an over packed suitcase full of fashionable size six summer wear.

Their ears rang, they were deaf for a moment or two – Dalton talked, but Lizzy heard nothing. Then with a kind of pop, she heard him, repeating, "What do we do? What do we do?"

"I'm guessing there's been a plane crash," Lizzy said, "And if what you see on CSI is right, you're not supposed to touch anything. However," she told him, climbing out of bed, and gingerly walking around glass and human remains, "I am for sure snagging the contents of that suitcase."

"But what about *her*?" Dalton said, pointing at the burning corpse in the armchair.

"I suppose you could pour water on her, just don't move her. Go look for something in the bath-room, a bucket or a vase – anything."

Dutifully, Dalton climbed out of bed in his boxers, and made his own careful way toward the bathroom. "Oh, my God," he said, and he gagged as if he prepared to vomit, "There's like – I mean – Jesus, someone's insides over here."

Lizzy spoke over her shoulder, as she gathered up all of the perfect, Parisian summer clothes and shoes and tossed them on the bed, "Just get something to stop burning woman, Dalton. Then we'll go check on everybody else." As he moved again to the bathroom door, Lizzy finished emptying the suitcase, and violating every *CSI* rule, picked up the Longchamps suitcase with a pillow case (she didn't want her fingerprints or DNA on it) and hurled it out the smashed window. Then, she gathered all her new clothes and shoes, purses and what-nots, inside the duvet – first pulling out a gorgeous pink and blue sundress and sandals – and stuffed her loot into the wardrobe, which unfortunately necessitated knocking someone's braceleted arm off the handles.

Meanwhile, Dalton reappeared with a giant pail he'd found and started pouring water over burning woman – she sizzled and smoked, which smelled disgustingly like a luau, kerosene tiki-torches and roast pork, but she kept on burning. "She's really hot," Dalton said. Then, "I don't mean like *that*, Jesus, I mean she's putting out heat like a stove."

"Human's burn like that," Lizzy said, taking her dress and shoes into the bathroom, "once they dry out and the fire gets the fat going. Don't worry about it. The chair's not going to burn, because I know Alex only buys EU approved products."

Dalton stood there watching the woman sizzle and smoke; then he looked out the window at the vista of fire, bodies and debris in trees, and the sounds from far and near of screams.

"Fuck me blind," he said.

"I'm going to change," Lizzy said, slamming the bathroom door. "Give me a minute."

A chronic insomniac, drunk from Alex and Laurent's superb wine collection, Sandrine had been smoking as she luxuriated in a hot bath. Her sleepy head had just lolled back against a towel when all Hell broke loose: noise, explosion, a suction so intense that it pulled her nightie right out the window, then a smell of kerosene and bright flames everywhere, and – splash – she was joined in the bathtub by the upper torso of a handsome young man, still wearing his shirt and tie, but minus everything below his waist. Sandrine stared at him for a moment, propped in the water at the other end of the bathtub, his hair charmingly mussed, and then she blew a cloud of smoke and climbed out of the tub saying, "Too fucking bad; he was a handsome guy."

Alex and Laurent slept soundly, cocooned together in their fashion. They awoke to some unknown thing that disturbed their sleep, and woke them up in time to hear the explosion, see the flames, watch their velvet drapes disappear through the *portes-fenêtres*, and then through the shattered glass the arrival of assorted and peculiar detritus: an airplane food cart, an airline window, an entire coach seat, with someone's midsection, minus torso and legs, firmly buckled in, and several pairs of mix-matched shoes.

"What makes such a —?" Laurent said groggily.

"Plane crash," Alex told him, pointing out the window toward the burning skyline of Godiche.

"Oh, *mon dieu* – the festival."

They looked at one another in horror; then looked again out the window in even greater horror.

"There is a woman's leg hanging from our drapery rod," Laurent said, gesturing.

"Perhaps one of those shoes is hers," Alex said, as they both got out of bed, searching fruitlessly for their robes.

"She has a nice leg," Laurent said, examining it. "Good form – young, I think."

"What I think is that we'd better throw some clothes on and go check on everyone and the house," Alex told him.

Laurent was peering out on the window at the inferno of Godiche. He sounded completely unlike himself – as if the inferno touched the deepest and most somber part of his soul. "This is unbelievably bad, Alex. *Unbelievably bad.*"

By dint of architectural design, they turned up around the same time in the grand lobby. Sandrine wore one of Alex and Laurent's enormous *Deschamps* bath towels as a sarong, since the explosion had sucked her nightie out the window. Lizzy, on the other hand, radiated Parisian chic, in a summer sun dress and sandals. When Alex cocked a curious eye at her, she shrugged and said with a quiet threat, "*Don't ask.*"

The men all wore a motley collection of hastily retrieved clothes. No one knew what to say. They simply stood in a clump, surveying the relatively undamaged house, decorated now – of course – with strange objects: books, shoes, eyeglasses, purses, luggage, hands, feet, heads, a dead and mangled poodle, fur still burning, and human gore of all hideous possibilities.

"We made a tour of the outside," Laurent said, breaking the silence, "and a half-naked flight attendant and her seat are – *qu'est-ce que ça veut dire?*"

"Embedded," Alex told him.

"*Voilà* – in the south wall."

"*Jesus H. Christ,*" Dalton said, still traumatized by the smoldering corpse in their room.

"Fucking stole my new nightie, that good one from Monoprix," Sandrine said.

"*The flight attendant?*" Dalton asked.

Sandrine looked at him, preparing her withering riposte. However, seeing his deathly pallor and understanding that he was in shock, she pulled him into a French-style embrace, causing her left boob to pop out from its *Deschamps* folds. Alex, Laurent, and Lizzy all noted her Sandrine performance; Dalton did not (something Sandrine *did* notice).

By now, the orange-red night had filled with ceaseless French sirens, and they heard and then saw through the blown-out oak doors, a military convoy chundering along their farm road toward the Dresden-esque firestorm that had once been Godiche. They moved to the doorway and began to step out for a better look, when the lights and rotors of two Air Force helicopters stopped them in their tracks and forced them to cower hurriedly just inside the door.

The rotor blades created a gale of body parts, clothing, items of every composition, including a blizzard of neatly wrapped first-class salads, which Sandrine clearly eyed up for salvage. When the wind settled down, Alex peeped around the corner and looked straight into the face of one of those high-ranking military officers who, in any country, mean business.

He saluted Alex, French style – in which citizens were always saluted – and asked him, "You are the owner?"

"Yes," Alex said, "We are," and he gestured toward Laurent – who appeared transfixed by watching his mother pilfer salads and hide them in her towel sarong.

"Belgian?" The officer asked.

"*No*," Alex said in indignation, "*American*."

"Superb French for an American."

"Thank you."

"Now," the officer said, "I am LeClerc, *Général de division aérien*, and we are commandeering this area," and he held a finger at their front yard, "for triage. Doctors and nurses should be arriving shortly from the base at Marans; they have a specialty burn unit. This is the only available house and property for at least a kilometer in any direction. He exploded up there," Général LeClerc said, looking up at their roof. "An Airbus 380, fully loaded."

"Fuck me blind," Lizzy said. "That's a lot of people."

"Not to mention the village," the Général said, looking worriedly in the direction of the inferno.

Sandrine gathered up more salads and wrapped desserts, though no one seemed to notice. More familiar than the French with catastrophes natural and unnatural, Alex, Lizzy and Dalton immediately grasped the significance to the layout of a field hospital – from the green, yellow, and red polyethylene sheeting, to the number of nurses in each locale.

They stood on the front steps and regarded the immense landscape as it quickly filled with medical personnel, cots, gurneys, drip tubes, rolling curtains, officious people with walkie-talkies and the non-stop roar of helicopter rotors. Someone had, by now, figured out just where to land and take off behind the wall between their property and Madame Chenevier's former melon field – now a jet-fuel desiccated desert.

Alex explained the colors to Sandrine and Laurent, "Dead or nearly; probably hopeless, but some hope; worth the extra effort because they should survive."

"Holy Hell," Dalton said, "Their body tags match those tarp things perfectly." Even in crises, French style asserted its influence: the elegant script on each color-coordinated tag, black on the red tags, and *bleue-marine* on the yellow, crisp white on the green.

"Can we help?" Lizzy asked the Général as he brisked by.

He turned, saluted, and said, "You could begin cataloging the human remains and objects – watches, rings, shoes – in the house, and you might comfort the walkers," he said. "We have an increasing number of those who somehow survived the blast and fire," and he shook his head as if he found it unbelievable. In many ways it was.

At that precise moment, the completely dazed, naked, and barefoot Mayor of Godiche appeared – clinging to an equally naked and barefoot, but tall, handsome, and remarkable specimen of manhood. Laurent whispered to the Général, "*Monsieur le Maire* and one of our local gendarmes, Lieutenant Alfred Meserve."

The Général gave a smart, sharp salute, "*Monsieur le Maire*," and then another, less sharp salute, "Lieutenant Meserve."

The Mayor simply stared, catatonic, but the gorgeous gendarme with six pack abs and long fit legs saluted back and said, "*Je tiens à vous exprimer notre gratitude, Général.*"

The Général offered him only a quick salute and nod.

"Come on," Lizzy said, in a different Lizzy voice than any of them had yet heard, taking the Mayor's hand, and leading their naked refugees toward the house. "Let's clean you up, find you some clothes," and she gestured at Dalton, meaning *you* find something from your backpack wardrobe to fit a broad-shouldered six-foot gendarme. "And let's see if we can find a nurse to look at your feet. "She glanced at the *Général*, who saluted her with a look that said, 'I'll find one immediately.'"

Sandrine shook her head and blew an enormous plume of smoke skyward; then she pointed her cigarette at a helicopter, and said, "What a Hell of a thing. *Huh?* Those Cheneviers had the best melons in the fucking Vendée. *Va te faire foutre*," she said to one of the plane's engines, which perched precariously in the branches of an oak tree – firemen still spraying it and arguing with soldiers about how to get it down. "*Va te faire foutre!*"

As Catatonic as he had been when arriving, *Monsieur le Maire* became as talkative while the nurse tended to his feet. He began a non-stop narrative about their survival – to the embarrassment of the gendarme, who turned scarlet as a tomato. He now wore one of Dalton's tank-tops and a pair of shorts – which looked fetching on him – and even bandaged, his feet fit into an old pair of Alex's house slippers.

Apparently, the two of them had just stripped off, preparatory to their scheduled romp in the Nazi-era bunker under the *Marie* basement – still filled with German memorabilia, including maps with the addresses of reliable collaborators, about which the town was chiefly (and intentionally) oblivious.

The mayor's sexuality had long been the subject of village speculation, Laurent told them, and he found the story riveting, sitting with his elbows on the table, staring at the gendarme, not the Mayor.

In any event, propped in the gendarme's strong arms, back against the bunker wall feet up around the gendarme's neck, the two of them shielded by a reinforced support, they were just getting into the good part when the *Mairie* exploded and collapsed. Somehow, they were unscathed – but above them loomed sky and flames, they heard screams of anguish. After a few moments of complete disorientation, they managed gingerly to make their barefoot way up and over all the assorted debris, dodging flaming things of all types.

In what had been the main lobby of the Mairie they found a broad empty floor, surrounded by massive walls of flames. The Marie burned fiercely, which included the Mayor's top floor apartment – with his wife and three little girls. Clearly, they were dead.

No one could have survived this holocaust, the heat and smoke from which were quickly driving the naked men out into what had been the street – but not before the Mayor made the horrible discovery of his daughters' three ravaged teddy bears (Sissy, Carla, and Rihanna), singed, and smoking.

In tears, the naked men made their way along the street, pushing aside the headless torsos, hurrying past the bodies burning in seats, avoiding look up at the collapsed and flaming remnants of the famed Summer Festival – including the incinerated grinning remnants of charred passengers, who still swung in Ferris wheel baskets.

The worst moments of the war could not have been like this. By instinct, by luck, they made their way out of the exploding *Centre de ville*, and ended up here, at Alex and Laurent's. The Mayor began sobbing uncontrollably, and looking up at no one, said in a shaking face, "Rihanna, my daughter Sophie's teddy bear – *she had no ears or eyes*."

At which moment, Sandrine made a puzzling murmur, and with a brutal crash passed out cold on the kitchen floor.

Roaming the house in the hope of finding – what? Dalton opened a door on a room of bawling children, some bandaged, and not an adult in sight. Every eye of every child turned to him, so Dalton rose to the occasion. In one of those moments, in which life suddenly makes sense, and in order to give the distressed children rides on his back he said to them – inexplicably, really – in a flawless replication of his High School French teacher, all of those years of *dictation* paying off. "*Je m'appelle* Dalton."

From that, they went ahead with a good half hour of increasingly exhausting rides on Dalton's back. Embracing as many of them as he could, he said, "I must stop now. I am fatigued, *mes chéries.*

"Thank you," a lovely, black-haired, green-eyed little girl said. "Can I speak with my maman or papa now, please?"

Dalton squeezed her in a tight hug, said he would see if he could locate them – and then he left the room in tears and went in search of a far-away room where he might finally be alone. On the third floor, at the south end, he opened a door on a room that he could at once tell had been the one prepared for the dead Kitty-Louise. A little hand-lettered sign said, "Bathroom through that door," with an arrow, and, "wardrobe there," with another arrow. Seeing that – perhaps because the room faced south? – the window was unbroken, Dalton tore the note to shreds, threw off his clothes and climbed into bed and fell into one of the soundest sleeps of his life.

CHAPTER

13

Lizzy had gone out into the backyard, to get some relief from the crowded, smelly house – not that the prevalent Godiche smell of smoke, roast pork and kerosene proved much better – when she stumbled the Mayor's friend. He sat on the ground, back against a tree. When he heard Lizzy and looked up, their eyes met in a kind of strangely synchronous union – impossible for Lizzy to explain in any other fashion. It was as if they had known one another all their lives, bizarre as that was.

She knelt beside him and said in French, "Are you all right?"

He shrugged.

She gestured to a spot next to him. "May I?"

"Yes, yes, of course."

She settled with her back against the tree, her bare arm against his. He still wore one of Dalton's tank tops. They sat like that in complete silence – save for the continuing warble of sirens, screams in the distance, and other noises of unknown origin. Only after the passage of too much time did Lizzy say, without looking at him. "I'm Lizzy, American. I'm here staying with my cousin and his partner – they're gay too."

He looked puzzled.

"I mean, you and the *Monsieur le Maire.*"

He smiled. "No, no – Monsieur le Maire, oh yes, *he* is gay. Me? No. I am just doing as I am told. It's a decent job and I – well, I mean ..."

"It's all right," Lizzie said, "It's one of the oldest and saddest stories in the world. No worries. I understand – *completely.*"

"Thank you, Lizzy. You are very – well, I am Nicolas," he said, turning his face with those I've-known-you-forever green eyes to her, "and this is the only house not hugely damaged or destroyed. I suppose you know that."

"Yes, because the plane exploded directly overhead. This is ground zero. So, the blast radiated out from," and she gestured toward the orange-red sky above the house, "there, sparing whatever was directly beneath it. Just luck, really – I mean, for us."

He nodded. "I never ..." but he couldn't continue. Falling silent, he leaned against her and then, quite normally – or at least that's how it felt to Lizzy – he took her hand and held it. She squeezed it, to show that she liked it.

"Where are you from?" she asked.

"Niort," he said. Then after a moment of shared silence, "I've been helping the pompiers tag bodies and body parts, the military is in charge now," and his tone of voice showed how he felt about it all. He held up his iPhone. "I tag the – piece or pieces, usually unrecognizable, sometimes still burning – and I photo them and then immediately send it to the military command. I have a specific color, so they can map everything correctly."

"Oh, my God," she said. "Nicolas, what a horrible thing you have to do."

He nodded. "I am quite traumatized, Lizzy."

She kissed the side of his head gently and leaned even more tightly against him. "Always will be, you know that."

"Yes. I know about post-traumatic stress. It often happens to soldiers, but not on this scale. Do you suppose it was like this for the firemen at the World Trade Center?"

"Yes," she said, "probably. Except they lost a lot of their friends, so – but, yes, similar."

"I wouldn't want someone to find my head in a rosebush, burning still and looking up with a scared last moment before …," he sighed. "Imagine that. We can't touch them, so I must let him burn. His head is just a burned-up bit of DNA with an identity flag and number."

"Actually, there's an entire body up in my bedroom," and she gestured toward the blown out *portes-fenetres* of her room. "It landed in a *fauteuil*, in a posture like Greta Garbo, corpse still smoking. Fortunately, the chair only burned a little. Alex and Laurent only buy the best stuff."

"EU fire retarding codes for furniture are very exacting," Nicolas said.

"Have you been in the military a long time?"

"Yes, ten years. It's a good career. I am twenty-seven. A bit sad these days already, since my fiancée left me for a woman – over a year ago, so really, I am over it. Just kind of sad always to be alone."

"Tell me about it," Lizzy said. "I'm sure others have said this, but it's best that she left you before rather than after – if she's lesbian."

"Oh, yes, no one blames her, even I do not. In fact, she did the honorable thing. But it doesn't make me less lonely."

"You're a handsome man," she said, "it can't be hard for you to meet someone else."

"Of course not," He shrugged. "But I believe in romance. That there must be a special spark – and the pickings are somewhat sparse in Niort and Godiche – not to mention my – let's say my obligations to *Monsieur le Maire*."

"Luckily, I don't have a problem with the Sioux City Mayor, other than that he's a Republican nitwit. Sioux City, that's where I live. In Iowa?"

He shrugged his ignorance about Iowa

"But, I'm the same way otherwise." It pleased her to be with a man who had never heard of her State, let alone her city. It felt liberating. "Do you have a big family?" she asked.

"No, my elder sister Annick, that is all. She is married and lives in Lyon."

"Oh, that's where Laurent is from. His mother owns some Laundromats there."

"My sister's husband is a lawyer and they live rather pretentiously, although I love her dearly. She can live as she wishes. Me, no, I am not pretentious. *Life* matters to me, not possessions. That's why this ...," and he pointed vaguely toward the burning remnants of Godiche.

"I hate pretension," Lizzy said, "though I agree with you that someone can be nice and be pretentious, like your sister. But in my family, people have tended to be pretentious and nasty. I could live anywhere, as long as I loved my man and he loved me back."

"Yes?" he said, turning those radar eyes on her once again, "That's exactly true for me, Lizzy – I could live anywhere, so long as I had the love of my *femme*."

At that precise moment, Lizzy knew that she wanted never to be apart from Nicolas – that she wanted to marry him, have his children, and to live in France. It came to her like a vision, true, complete, undeniable. In his stunning green eyes, she saw the same mirrored feelings.

He brought his face closer to her, and then he kissed her, and she kissed him back – and they continued to kiss for a long while.

CHAPTER

14

Only after a long and fretful search through the triage compound that had been their beautiful woods and gardens – with the persistent intrusions now of international media, who did *not* heed the President's call for the nation to stay calm and, as importantly, far away from the scene of the disaster – did Laurent find his mother.

She was in the area reserved for the dying and, now, the mind-boggling number of dead. When he found her, she was with a dying little boy, burned over so much of his body that death would be a blessing. Amid so much roasted, charred, bloated flesh, his face alone seemed untouched. He seemed at peace, staring with big black eyes at Sandrine.

She lay next to him and sang, softly and sweetly, in a voice Laurent had not heard since he has a youngster. Tears ran down her face, as periodically she kissed her young patient, as he formed words like, "Maman," and "Fritzi?" Sandrine had decided to sing the children's folksong, "*À Paris sur mon petit cheval gris.*"

Her sweet voice, so close to what was left of his ear, sang a song he clearly knew – as his lips tried to smile from time-to-time. "*To Paris, to Paris, On my little grey horse, To Rouen, to Rouen, On my little white horse, To Toulon, to Toulon, On my little blond horse, And let's go back to the manor house, On my little black horse. At a gallop, at a gallop –* "

Laurent saw the change come over the boy's face, and then the vapid glistening of his eyes. The nurse, who had been hovering in the shadows, bent down – revealing that she also cried – and she said to Sandrine, "He has gone, Madame."

Sandrine closed his eyes for him, sat up, brushed herself off – dead skin and burnt clothing – and then she stood and noticed Laurent. They stared at one another – Laurent expecting a 'What a fuck of a thing' at any moment – and then she pulled him into a tight embrace, and sobbing said to him through her tears, "My boy, my precious boy."

"I'm here, *Maman.* I'm here."

She looked him again in the face. "I shall never again smoke another cigarette," she said, with a brisk wave at the field of smoking death, "and as God is my witness, I shall never swear again

– *never.*" Then she burst into further sobs and grabbed Laurent in their hug.

Alex found them at the moment of their emotional profusion and simply stared, utterly confounded by the scene.

All three of them regarded one another. "The General would like to speak with us; however, I can't find Dalton or Lizzy. I suspect she's in her room with the key in the lock because I tried to go in, but there's no sign whatsoever of Dalton.

"*Bon*," Sandrine said, wiping her eyes, "the three of us shall speak with *M. le General*." She turned back one final time to look at the lifeless boy, and blowing him a kiss said, "Goodnight, *mon petit ange*; sleep well with the angels."

Alex looked at weeping Laurent, took him in his arms, and thought that this experience would so forever change all their lives that – in the end – it would amount to basically starting over.

For either or long brief time – he never could recall – Byron stood in his boxers with a deep but self-cauterized wound and stared uncomprehendingly. The air was unbreathable. From every side came screams and cries of pain, people calling out for help or for other people by name, and equally came explosions and more intense infernos of flame.

He looked down at the ground where a human hand, still attached to most of its arm pointed toward the road that went northwest out of the town center. For some unknown reason, that severed fortune-telling hand, knocked him from his certain-death reverie and awoke him to the knowledge that he must find his way to the house they passed by yesterday.

He began walking, as best he could, in that direction. After a few minutes he no longer thought about what he walked on, only avoiding sharp metal or anything on fire. The air was so hot that it seemed to be sucking out the oxygen he needed to breath – and recalling something he had read about the firestorms in Dresden during World War II, he understood what was about to happen. His years of track and running saved his life. He tilted forward and ran with every *sliver* of energy toward the road out of town, so fast that he did remember – even years and events later – that he would certainly have won a medal in competition for that life or death run. In any event as he reached the limit of his ability and had passed beyond the last bit of village, he felt the gigantic suction of the firestorm.

Clinging to a stop sign, as gale-force winds whipped by him to fuel the cyclone of fire, what remained of Godiche became a swirling red-orange tornado of flame. He stared at the almost beautiful swirling fire tower, as if the village and all of those in it were merely one flick of a cosmic match. He watched flames devour a news helicopter from Switzerland in a quick explosion, and then a vague thunk as it hit the street.

Finding his breathing again becoming labored, he turned and began walking toward the Northwest.

At first, he saw no one else, just carnage of a mindboggling kind and quality. His leg had belatedly started to hurt, and bending down to look at it, he saw a shard of metal imbedded there. While Byron had never gone to medical school, he knew enough to be careful – he didn't know if it was just in muscle or if it had severed a vein or major artery and was now staunching the blood loss. He calculated the odds and pulled it out.

The puckered wound seemed to have cauterized itself on impact, and it stopped hurting and oozed some fluid that did not look like blood. As he was standing back up to continue his trek along the road, he heard someone calling out. As far as he could tell, it came from a pile of rubble beside what must have been a melon field and orchard.

Trees – of unknown fruit – burned with the wicked determination of oil-soaked Tiki torches.

He made his way off the road, which meant climbing over a stone and putting his foot straight down on what remained of a woman's carbonized severed head. For a moment he thought he was going to retch, he tasted that bile in his mouth, but he didn't – chiefly because his eyes had caught sight of a shirt, flapping from the remains of a chicken coop, filled now with smoldering overcooked hens. He grabbed the shirt, saw the size – a French 41 –

and he had a winner, a pale blue Lacoste, button down shirt, neither bloodied nor damaged, so it must have been well packed in a nice suitcase – which, unfortunately, seemed *not* to be in the vicinity.

Again, the voice called out, and reminded of his chore, Byron moved across a brick area and peered into the stones. An elderly woman looked at him, from where she was crushed beneath wood, stones, and slates.

Byron knelt and touched her face,

"*Mon chien,*" she said pointing, « *Je vous en supplie, sauvez mon chien, il est un bon garçon, et il sera fidèle et va vous protéger.* »

At the sound of her speech, a beautiful golden Labrador moved toward Byron, growling and snarling, teeth bared. But the old woman spoke quietly to him and pointed at Byron.

"*Il s'appelle?*" Byron asked, thinking it best to know his new companion's name.

"Lapin," she said, and at his name the dog stopped his growling and wagged his tail. In French, the woman said, "It's his favorite dinner. Now, you go with the nice man, go – and take care of him for me," she implored Byron.

Lapin looked from the woman to Byron, and when Byron beckoned to him the dog licked the woman's face and made some whimpers, and then he moved toward Byron and held his body tight against Byron's leg. Together they made it to the wall, and Lapin passively allowed Byron to lift him

up and over, but they had no sooner started walking toward the lights and activity that Byron spotted as they made a turn that the stone pile behind
them erupted in a huge explosion of flame, knocking Byron flat on his face.

CHAPTER

16

With the help of Lapin, Byron managed to find a good pair of shoes and some trousers – which might have blown out of one of the destroyed houses along the road. They didn't have the look of trousers one would take on vacation. However, he wasn't complaining. So, presentably clad, he and Lapin – who held tightly to Byron's right leg – made their way toward Alex and Laurent's house.

They knew the house was nearby, because they heard and saw the multiple helicopters, stepped out of the way of Doppler-wheedling ambulances, and smelled the lack of kerosene from that direction. It seemed ever so far, however. Both he and Lapin had grown exhausted, when a man – clearly crazed from the experience, and severely burned, appeared from nowhere and lunged at Byron with a huge kitchen knife.

Had it not been for the quick intervention of Lapin, Byron would have died then on the road toward safety. However, Lapin leapt at the man, knocked him over, clamped his jaw on the man's arm – until screaming he released the knife. He lay hurling epithets as Byron and Lapin made their last push toward Alex and Laurent's.

Stopping to catch his breath at the gate to the house, Byron saw the diminishing paraphernalia of death. Lapin, too, must have sensed the horror, because he weaved in between Byron's legs as if to ward off even the incinerated specters of this carnage. They watched as, stepping out of the way, strangely clad men in protective suits pulled up in vans and stopped on the lawn.

Byron thought later how he hadn't thought of his brother. He thought about himself. He looked out on the scene, the house, and every wish, hope, dream he'd ever had washed over him.

"I'm gay," he said to Lapin.

Lapin made a noise of approval.

"Everyone's known it but me."

He remembered his last morning in the apartment before his marriage. Genuine, the smell of coffee and a Cimmerian sky through a dirty window. It howled with memory, childhood itself. It touched inner visions. Reminders of things past swirled up with that coffee aroma, tinctures of childhood, released through the phantom shapes which played against the glass.

But what had Byron seen anyway, except his reflection in the window, and a light on a balcony across the courtyard? Yet it seemed utterly real, without compromise. He sipped his coffee, hands cupped around the mug. When he blew on the surface, he felt a moist hot sensation against his eyelids, and he thought that – most of all – he needed to relax.

Relax? *Frankie Goes to Hollywood?* Oh, God. He had leaned back in his chair and looked at the kitchen ceiling. More there to see, crevices, spider webs, grease marks, but it was not the conundrum of shadows through glass. He moved forward again and peered into the morning. In his reflected eyes he saw a twenty-seven-year-old man shadowed by his sense of waiting – but waiting for what?

And now he knew – looking up toward the country manse of Alex and Laurent. He had been waiting for this.

"*On y va,*" Byron said to Lapin. "I'll get you some water, find you something to eat – and then we'll both find a place in that house to sleep."

Lapin barked his approval.

Exhausted as he was – traumatized and yet curiously liberated, Byron managed to open the front door make his way by instinct to the kitchen (banging his shin once, but at this point what was one shin more or less). He felt himself to be in a sort of race with the men in Hazmat suits who were gathering now in force on the front lawn.

He found a bowl, filled it to the brim with water – to which Lapin leapt like a beast who'd been wandering the Sahara – and then opening the refrigerator, scrounged around until he found a leg of lamb. Seeing that Lapin had finished his water, with his water bowl and lamb leg, Byron led the one man, one dog parade upstairs. Clearly, the bedrooms on this floor were all in use – they either had signs demanding peace or those inside had locked the door.

He went up to the third floor and found the situation the same there – only now he began to worry, but at last, on the fourth floor he struck pay dirt – an unlocked door at the far end of the corridor. He opened it and stood for a moment startled – well, more than that – stupefied. The man Byron would most love to love – or rather, the kind of man he would most want to love *him*, was sprawled on top of the bed in his boxers, blond, hairy-chested, muscled.

Tossing the lamb leg at last to a famished Lapin, Byron used the toilet, filled Lapin's water bowl, stripped all his tainted and smelling clothes off and climbed on to the bed. The Adonis next to him never flinched. So, with a sense of now or never, Byron managed to maneuver one of the man's arms around Byron's shoulder so that Byron could sleep in the crook of his Adonis shoulder. Then he stretched his hand out across the naked chest, curled tightly against this stranger, put his right leg over the sleeping man's leg and then down between the two strong legs – and within a matter of seconds he had ejaculated everywhere and fallen asleep like a baby.

They awoke at precisely the same moment, two strangers in a big comfortable bed in a third floor, south-facing guest room – the one farthest from everyone else. Of course, on first waking they merely stared at one another – but somehow it was vastly more complex than staring at one another. The sun awakened them, shining directly into one set of eyes and the happenstance reflection of that same sun in the mirror on the wardrobe. Neither could ever remember how long they simply stared, eyes into eyes, until -- at the same moment – entirely spontaneously – they both reached up to touch the other's face. A small gasp from each of them as they realized how much they liked what they felt, and as each knew – strange as life was – that they had just fallen in love.

As if he had done it all his life, Dalton took his new love's face in his hands and kissed it with such fervent masculine passion, that within a matter of moments they were making love with the passion of wild animals. Fueled by the intensity of last night's events, Byron and Dalton proceeded to introduce one another to sex. It was as if Byron had always known that this was what he wanted – to be the bottom, the gay recipient of another man's ardor. Certainly, the two of them – having by now exchanged names and declared their love – continued to perform acrobatics neither had ever imagined – not even from college porn flicks, not from gossip or books.

In fact, to both of them their previous sex seemed now to have been mechanical, and Dalton saw it with utter Coleridge-style opiate dreaming, and Byron realized that *this* – this hairy-chested, enormous man – was what he had been waiting for all his life. In truth, neither could begin to describe it – even after the many later decades of their marriage, and three adopted children – and would ever after hold this inexplicable orgy as their model for true love.

Mind you, Byron's sincere adoration of Dalton's penis made Dalton pull ape sex out of his ancestral memory – because it fueled his drive like nitroglycerin. It wasn't safe sex, and after that day they remained monogamous – but considering they had survived a catastrophe now non-stop headline news around the world, neither of them really gave a damn about safe or not safe.

As they prepared for their third go at it, Byron kissed Dalton's penis and held it loving against his face, the same penis about which Kandy once said, "It needs reduction surgery or something, Dalton, it's too thick and long." The same penis to which Byron whispered, "You are my world, my world – *my world.*"

Alex was busily trying to make as much sense of the morning as he could. Neither he nor Laurent had made it up to bed, so they were fueled now only by coffee and adrenaline. All through the night they had helped where they could and stayed out of the way as much as they were able, as with thorough efficiency men and women in Hazmat suits took away everything even vaguely human in origin and carefully photographed and bagged every piece of material they felt it necessary to collect.

Thus, Laurent cried non-stop as men in suits carted away so many of his clocks and valuable pieces in sheer latex wrapping. Toward morning, efficient soldiers removed the last of the patients and corpses, as Alex and Laurent sat and watched the sunrise, surveying from their kitchen window the miles of smoking devastation. When a mighty clanking shook the window, they knew that the flight attendant, whom they had collectively and affectionately nicknamed "*Rasée*," due to her shaved crotch, had finally been brought down.

They both turned as Sandrine walked into the room in her back-up nightie, kissed them both and said softly, "All the same, God is good to us."

In all the time he had known Laurent, Alex had never heard him utter a harsh word to Sandrine. He had that French adoration of his mother. So, when Laurent leapt up and said, "*God?* What shit. *Good to us?* But not to all those *others*," and he waved over the abandoned lawn.

Alex was on his feet before he realized he intended to speak. "How *dare* you talk to your mother in this fashion," he said in French.

Laurent crumpled. If it had been the first occasion on which Alex heard Laurent berate his mother, then it had also been the first time that Alex raised his voice or spoke in that sharp French tone to Laurent. The three of them stood in silence, glaring and staring.

"We are French, Laurent. God is a concept to us. We are not hootenannies from Alaska," Sandrine growled.

"You mean Hillbillies from Nebraska – but I think that Nebraska is not from where they come either," Laurent said in a soft and repentant voice.

Sandrine waved a hand in dismissal. "My remark meant that the sun has risen, we are alive;

we have food and work." She paused and Alex saw her jaw tense; he thought she was going to curse. However, she reached into the pocket of her robe and pulled out a pearl earring. "My little dying angel gave it to me. It is his mother's. He filched it last year to hold for good luck, and he said to me. 'But if my *maman* is gone, then you keep it. I would like you for a mother."

Tears welled up in Sandrine's eyes. Again, they stood in silent confusion.

Sandrine slapped the back of Laurent's head in a gentle gesture, but not one with a gentle message. "Speak to me again like that," she said, "and they'll need to call in the gendarmes. *Understood?*"

"Understood." Laurent blinked away tears. "Yes, *Maman*." Then he looked at Alex and asked, "Please forgive me, Alex."

Alex went to him and held Laurent in strong, reassuring arms, and kissed his cheek. "I love you," he said.

"*Monsieur* Dalton," a little girl said, peeking her head around the door. "We're very hungry, and no one came for us."

Dalton and Byron had only just finished making their most passionate bout of love yet, and having sworn undying love, marriage, and an eternity together, were lying in one another's sweat. Byron was about to discover yet another astonishing feature of the man of his life.

Dalton said, "Who are *us*? I know you are Sylvie, but – "

A little boy's three-year old face peered around the door beneath Sylvie's, "It is I, *Monsieur* Dalton."

"Ah, Lionel. Come in, come in. This is soon to be one of your papas. His name is Byron."

The French children looked at one another, puzzling out such a bizarre name. Then, Sylvie said, "*Bonne matin, Monsieur* Belfort."

Little Lionel, blond hair ruffled, bowed, "Are you *Monsieur* Dalton's husband?"

"Yes – well, soon. Yes."

Both clapped their hands.

In a surprisingly lighthearted tone, Dalton said, spreading his hands beatifically over the children, "They are from the orphanage – which the – well, it ..."

"And now you get to live with us," Byron said, with a pause of breathy anticipation. "*In New York.*"

The children first looked shocked, then excited, then they danced in a circle holding hands as Lapin barked and danced with them. As they danced, Dalton and Byron had a quick confab.

"Little Lionel, no one would adopt because of the harelip and his teeth."

Byron looked shocked. "We can have them fixed in no time – oh, good Lord. No problem."

"And little Sylvie, as you've noticed, is of mixed race."

"I can tell you this," Byron said, "She'll be a beautiful woman – and our last name, Byron-Countryman. Has a ring to it, don't you think?"

"What are you talking about?" Sylvie asked.

"About you," Dalton bellowed, and then both jumped on the bed and into his waiting arms.

"Oh, you need a bath, *Monsieur* Dalton," Sylvie said.

"Blame *Monsieur* Byron," Dalton laughed.

"And this, Dalton told Byron, is our son Lionel." He gave Byron a kiss on his cheek, still holding the children and said, "Sadly, we all lost our papers in the crash, so we'll get evacuated, and once in New York," he glanced at Byron.

"Ah, my part." Byron held out his arms and Sylvie leapt into them. "My family who makes all things come right."

"Damn straight," Dalton said, with a fatherly smile. "Ain't no one messin' with my family. "And I'm thinking a big wedding – with no guns or suicides, and the two cutest flower whatever-you-call-'ems in history."

And to that Lapin thumped his tail and barked in happiness.

She felt his absence the instant she awoke still awash in male pheromones and sweat.; turning she saw the telltale signs of stealthy departure, except somehow, she knew he had not done a runner. It wasn't in Nicolas' nature. Having always described female intuition as 'a crock,' she believed in it where Nicolas was concerned. She picked up the carefully folded note on his pillow, and snap-flapped it open: "I tried to awaken you, but you slept too soundly," he wrote in his exquisite French Lycée handwriting. "So, I surrendered and wrote this letter, which is smothered in kisses and heaped with imaginary roses."

French to the bone, he had even made his side of the bed, which saddened her. She leapt from her side, went to the window, and saw several enormous helicopters taking off from the front lawn, faces peering from the little windows. She could have sworn she saw Dalton sitting beside one of the children, but it must have been her imagination. She climbed back into bed then, cuddling her lover's pillow, and drifted slowly back to sleep.

When she awoke someone had knocked on her door.

"Yes?" she called out.

"You've got the key in the lock," she heard Alex say.

"Oh, sorry," and climbing from bed, Lizzy draped the sheet around her and went to remedy the door situation.

Alex looked utterly exhausted, his face ashen, his eyes drained. His night had been different from hers, that was clear. He stepped a few feet into the room, which smelled of a strange combination of jet fuel and sex. Then he said, "Okay. My mom dropped dead in front of me on the day she arrived."

Lizzie wondered why on earth they were revisiting that at a time when hundreds, possibly thousands had died. She gave him a quizzical look.

"Never mind, I had a whole story composed, but to Hell with it. Most of the story is far too complicated for me to remember at the moment, Liz, but in a nutshell, someone shot the Chairman from Sunshine Airlines this morning – as well as the man who had just walked into the room, apparently on some assignment."

"*Nicolas*," she cried out.

"Nicolas. He had left word with his sister that you should be contacted if – *well*."

At first, Lizzie felt a surge of pragmatism, in which she worried (in that primordial intuitive animal fashion), "Who will take care of the twins? I can't raise them on my own because she knew she was pregnant, knew she was in shock, knew she would suffer from years of Post-Traumatic Stress. Pain she felt next, that she expected – television, film, YouTube, streaming videos of trains destroying school buses made her generation privy to the vivid morbidity of death.

She and Alex stared into and – *somehow* – though each other. Then they were in one another's arms, crying on mutual shoulders, Lizzy because she was in shocked horror and Alex because he was so far beyond tired and sick at heart that he cried because crying was runner up to self-immolation.

Then Lizzy did something neither she nor Alex would ever have imagined of her. She screamed as women scream in horror films; ironically, after a night like the one they'd just lived through, no one else in the house made a move – except a Hazmat officer who glanced quizzically over at them from the top of the stairs. Lizzy shook her head no; this was not something that easily fixed.

Bounding downstairs, utterly famished, Byron ran straight into his mother on the second-floor landing.

"What *are* you *wearing*?" she asked.

"*Mother*? How on earth did you get here."

"That pales in the face of my question. I can get into everywhere, including the Casino in Monte Carlo. *What* are you wearing?

"Some things I found in an old wardrobe – rather retro. A vintage look. Have you seen outside? There's been a a catastrophe, mother. How did you get here?"

She shrugged. "You father plays golf with the French Ambassador when he finds time and gets down to Washington. He made a few calls, there was a helicopter with the cutest Frenchman, who agreed not to turn the thing on until I was in-side."

"Why not?"

"My hair, Byron, does not do wind nor rain nor sleet nor whatever. He knew right where to come and landed smack in the front of this – if you don't mind me saying, rather dilapidated house." She pulled him into an awkward hug. "*I was so wor-ried, darling.* What mother wouldn't do this?"

Only my mother, Byron thought, would find a way to get here, wearing a designer suit, expen-sive shoes, and jewelry. Truth he told, he had never loved her mother more. Every Teddy grievance van-ished. "Mother – I'm in love, though not with Char-lotte, she died horribly in a restaurant. I made it safely here."

"Oh, *the poor dear*," she forced herself to say, while thinking of ways to avoid going to the fu-neral. She had never taken to Charlotte's family, which was all for the better. "But, I'm thrilled, sim-ply thrilled. I can't wait to tell your father. Is it a French – "

Dalton leaping down the stairs in full ath-letic glory, shirtless and wearing some ancient trousers and suspenders interrupted her. With the light from the landing window on his sun-bleached hair and chest, his shoulders, his height, he had never looked better. He grabbed Byron, lifted him up off his feet and gave him what Virginia Wild-wood thought an cinema-worthy passionate kiss.

"No, American. Mom, my soon-to-be husband Dalton – Dalton, my mother."

Years of training in the art of dealing with unexpected situations kept Virginia upright, smiling and even pulling this tall, scrumptious, sweaty man into a sincere hug – after all, Byron's sexuality had never been a surprise to her. "Such a *lovely* name for a son-in-law," she said, disengaging herself from his sweaty body before it destroyed her Dior scent. She gave them each a kiss on the cheek and said, "As soon as we get phone service in this – wasteland – I can't wait to tell your father."

Dalton and Byron couldn't keep their hands off one another and were locked in a sexually enticing embrace. Since Dalton stood now on a lower stair, Byron said over Dalton's naked shoulder and suspender strap:

"Guess where Dalton comes from, mother. No – you'll never guess. Sioux City, Iowa. Can you believe it."

Virginia felt jetlag and nuttiness causing her social skills to slide, so she quickly said, "Is there a powder room handy? And then I'd better find these young men Alex and Laurent." She started to turn but stopped. "By the way, we're off and away in an hour so if you've anything to pack or bring have it ready."

"Just Lapin, our dog," Dalton said, "And my Byron – and the two little orphans we're adopting."

At that moment, Virginia's phone rang. She looked at it as if it were demonic. French authorities had told her there would be no service here for days. "Oh, hello darling," she said, having failed to see who was calling. "Ah. Ah. Oh, dear. Yes, quite right. Use the florist on Park, that one on Lex overcharges. Well, he and his fiancé Dalton — yes, Dalton as in male." A moment of listening then, "Live with me being right, and tell the Country Club how happy you are. Right. That's my boy. Oh yes, handsome, tall and as manly as Cousin Cecily; he and Byron are standing right here," she muted the phone and said to Byron.

"It's your father. They found at least part of Kieran, including his passport."

"Kieran your Assistant?"

"How many others might their be?"

"He's here, poppet – or rather was here – doing some spy work for me. Sent me the most boring photos of you and Charlotte daily. Did I see her eating fast food? In France? Anyway, the poor man managed to go through the blades of a Rolls-Royce plane engine." Shaking her head at the two young men as if somehow it were Kieran's fault that he allowed an engine to suck him into it, and thinking about how she would handle this gay marriage for the greater good of the family, she put the phone into Byron's hand and inadvertently said out loud, "Go on the offensive, act as if everything is normal, and – "

"*What?*" Byron asked.

"I'm thinking out loud, Anyway, boys, hurry, hurry, I need to speak with your father about – " and she pointed at Lapin.

"Lapin," Byron said.

"Charming," she murmured, "and your two adoptees, which are something of an obstacle, though not one over which your father cannot hurdle." Listening to Byron speak about the situation to his father in French, clearly so that he could explain things without his Sioux City fiancé understanding. Well, she thought with pride – after all, *he is our son.* Then, she realized that she needed to phone Kieran's' mother, who probably didn't have the information yet about him.

It struck Virginia mightily, as she had only ever been struck before by the televised immolation of her son Teddy. Leaning over the bannister she vomited, and then she burst into tears and pulled her son into her arms – thinking of her last conversation with Kieran, whom she had sincerely liked and intended advancing skyward in her empire.

Byron, still on the phone with his father, had never seen his mother either cry *or* vomit in public. As she dragged Byron into her grip, he handed the phone to Dalton, saying. "Talk about sports, he always likes that." She put her hands in her hair, sighed, and said, "It's times like this that I miss Teddy the most. He was – never mind, it's irrelevant, *like most of my life.*"

Right on cue, they heard Dalton talking about the latest Stanley Cup and yachting news. Oh yes, Byron thought, those two will do fine together."

Leaning on the window ledge, Lizzy willed herself to cry – to gnash her teeth, to wail, but instead she simply felt ever weaker and lonelier. She knelt and then lay on her back, staring at the ceiling.

She heard rustling and turning her head, saw that Laurent was on the floor beside her. They met eyes; he took her hand.

"None of the windows in this gigantic room are broken," Lizzy said.

"That one is cracked," he said with French precision, and he pointed across the room – which ran the width of the house – "but these things are," and as far as possible he shrugged, "What is Alex's word that I love?"

"Serendipitous."

"*Et voilà*," he said.

"Why is this room so big?" She asked.

"School room," he said, "up until the twenties according to the records. The governess lived down at the end of the end of hall and then various senior servants along the corridor."

She thought a moment. "The other servants?"

He pointed upward. "There's a stairway, hidden behind that horse art and wainscoting."

"Is there heat up there?"

"Oh yes," he smiled, "little coal grates in small fireplaces, and in the summer – *alors*, the little dormer windows open – *sometimes*."

Finally, a few tears gathered in her eyes and she closed them against what she knew to be the ensuing storm.

"So," Laurent said, bringing her hand to his lips, "Since you are officially registered now as my fiancée. I want you to remain in France, and I think you wish it too."

She said nothing at first, letter tears run down her face. "But how –?"

He gave her a certain sort of look.

"Ah. Your mother."

"She has satchels full of Halal first class dinners and – well," he shrugged, "she's my mother."

They stared at long at one another, and still holding hands, she kissed his.

"We will need to make everything legal at the Prefecture as soon as possible. They are very fussy about these things."

Lizzie rolled over and pulled Laurent's arm around her. "If – "

"*If?*"

"I mean, if I am pregnant, and I probably am – and probably with twins – how will I ever," she leaned her face into his shoulder and smelled the beautifully fragrant alien soap. "I mean, everyone back home already knows about you and – "

Laurent laughed. "We will adopt the baby, babies, piglets, Alex and I – and then you shall be their Auntie Elisabeth, who lives here if she chooses or in Paris or – well, you will be officially married to me, a Frenchman so," he kissed her forehead, "Europe is your oyster."

CHAPTER

21

Virginia's limo glided to a stop and she was
ushered out and in, up a flight of stairs to one
of those absurdly modernistic dressing rooms, like
a cross between Arnold Schzwarnegger's *The Ter-*
minator and Christopher Robin's sitting room: an
array of absurdly frightening flowers, comforting
toast points and fresh caviar, bright blue-green
bottles of Slovenian mineral water.

Someone scrambled off in confusion.

A director babbled at her, a make-up person
blotted and wiped. Eyes saw her, as if these were
the moments before death – Marie Antoinette in
her tumbrel, as they took her to the guillotine.
They showed her an outline, but she did not even
try to read it. Someone gently took her arm and led
into another room. It was comfortable, had several
cameras and camera operators, stuffed chairs.

There was a backdrop, which looked like an Italian villa. In fact, she and Fred stayed in a villa on Capri once, and the view from the living room had an uncanny resemblance. She almost heard again the sounds of children on the rocks below. Her interviewer hurried in, all sympathy and concern, which surprised her. She mumbled something unkind about the tabloid press and referred to *Good Morning, America*, which baffled Virginia, since she had never heard of the show. They shook hands; she asked Virginia if she minded talking about her husband and extended family. Of course, not, she said. How exactly did Virginia want her to manage the tabloid material?

She shrugged. "Honestly," She suggested.

"What counts as honesty?" the interviewer asked.

They laughed.

"We'll be recording this," she reminded Virginia, "it's not really live. It can be edited – if necessary."

"It will not need to be edited," Virginia said.

"Right, then. Are you ready?"

"You bet," Virginia said.

"Maybe we could start with your signature smile?"

Virginia smiled at the camera.

"That's it," she said.

"That's it," Virginia agreed.

"Some smile."

"Thanks."

She leaned forward. "Your parents. Famous. The Hedgpeths. Wealthy. Powerful. Their names opened doors."

"Whether they wanted them open or not."

"Excuse me?" The interviewer said in confusion

"People try to please my parents, but they often wish – well, just to do a little shopping at Bloomingdales like anyone else." She did her Virginia smile again.

"But you have to admit, your family has mythic proportions – Senators, a Governor, Boards of Directors, well – the list would be endless."

They both laughed.

"Your sister's death?" the interviewer said. "It must still affect you – I mean, after all – "

"Suicide's hard to come to grips with. So mean hearted. Cruel. However, my sister was not mean hearted, and she was not cruel. I think she – well, changed toward the end. I do not think any of us will ever know why she did it. She just did."

"You were there. Could you describe that day for me?"

"There's not much to say about it, is there?"

"Let me ask you about the crash of Sunshine Air – when you heard about it, you must have been –?"

"Distraught. However, the French were magnificent about keeping families informed. I knew within a day that my son was alive."

"Your daughter-in-law died in the village – as they were eating?

"They were – well, yes, something like that."

"Your son has found himself tossed about in the tabloid press recently. Care to speak about that?"

Nice segue, Virginia thought. "Yes, of course," she said.

"Any truth in the – stories? It's been suggested that, well, he's – involved," she said gingerly, as if that might not be the word she meant to use. Her eyes seemed to drift off toward the director a moment, and

then she followed up by saying, "There was a photograph. Well, he has fallen in love with a man named Dalton Prescott from Iowa, and they have custody of two orphans? One reads that you and our husband are planning an enormous wedding."

"Enormous? Well, I don't know. The reception shall be enormous. It's a beautiful story of love and caring, and we think Dalton is a marvelous son-in-law. Therefore, I think one must examine the motives of the tabloid press. Look at why they print such things. They don't print such things because they really think selflessness and true love matter. Not at all. Scandal sells papers, my son being gay and falling in love and adopting orphans – well, it helped the papers turn a profit. It doesn't mean anything to them beyond the profit margin."

"But don't you agree that it's a most unusual story?" the interviewer asked, keeping them on task. "Wouldn't you like to talk about your son, Byron? About this huge wedding? About his partner from Iowa and the adopted children?"

Virginia looked at her, for an unguarded instant, as if she were a moron.

"Refuting stories about the details of suicide or discussing my son's private life isn't something well-bred people do."

"You agreed to appear this morning." The interviewer seemed completely puzzled.

"Well, comes a time one must make a statement – a public acknowledgement, or the stories grow ever meaner and more menacing."

"Some people think they go too far. The tabloids. Do you? Some people think they hurt people. Is that what you think?"

Virginia took a deep breath, trying to keep her signature smile glued to her face. "Yes, if you recall, the tabloids were what I wished to discuss."

"What about you what they've said about you?" interviewer woman asked.

"That's where I stay above the fray. I'm not going to talk about that, not any of it, I'm not going to discuss any aspect of my family's private life or my feelings about those – well, those suggestions about my feelings toward my sister Olivia."

"But she did commit suicide at your son's wedding – and now he's marrying a man and adopting children. You must admit it's quite the story."

"The story is in the fact that my son nearly died – the story is not in my sister's lesbian tendencies." Virginia kept smiling though inwardly she cursed; she rarely made a slip of the tongue, but when she did it invariably crackled.

The interviewer's eyes grew wide as saucers. Sweat seemed to break out on her upper lip. "So, you're saying that your sister, a fixture of the New York social scene was a lesbian?" She could hardly hold her excitement; her mind saw stations playing her interview endlessly. She was making her name, this instant; she was herself becoming famous, the next Barbara Walters perhaps.

"I'm not saying anything about it," Virginia reiterated.

"But isn't that the same thing?" she pursued.

"Why on earth is it the same thing?"

"All you have to do is refute the assertion."

"I don't want to refute the assertions."

"Silence is usually taken to be agreement."

"By whom?"

"The public."

"Why should the public care about my sister camping in Maine and hiking – oh, whatever mountain that was. I mean, really. I accept that my son's wedding to Dalton will be news – but is it really the public's business?"

"Your life is public domain."

"Why?"

"Because your family is famous."

"Why does being famous make my life public domain?"

"So, you're not going to deny the reports of your sister's death in a chapel after shooting the testicles off statues or her lesbianism or your son's upcoming gay marriage of the decade?"

"I have discussed it – all of it. So, I think it's time to talk about relief funds, contact numbers for the French consulate – not my family's private life."

"I think," the interviewer told the camera, "that Virginia Wildwood is not going to deny the recent tabloid stories about her son Byron's love affair with a Chicago commodities trader."

With a decisively noticeable sigh, Virginia took one last look at the phony Italian villa, and the make-believe view from a make-believe window, and thought through her smile, "The things I goddamned do for my family."

Virginia and the interviewer looked at one another.

"A very handsome and I dare say all-American Chicago commodities trader, who was the star of his Independent School soccer team," Virginia said, family pride having made her decide to give this pretty interviewer a kick in the crotch with an all-American fairy tale. "In fact, I think any mother would simply *love* having a son-in-law as tall, handsome, broad-shouldered, big-chested and heroic as Dalton."

After a moment of vaguely befuddled pause, her interviewer said. "Thank you."

"No," Virginia said, "Thank *you*,"

"Oh – well – of course, I mean – "

"Thank you for providing me a glimpse into your world – *this world* – the world as most people see and hear it." She shook her head, smiled that famous smile, and said in impeccable French, "*On peut se jester dans la guele du loup.*" Then in English, "And survive."

On her way out of the building, Virginia felt a puzzling wave of compassion; she stopped in the hallway and thought she was having morning sickness, which was impossible – unless the Immaculate Conception struck twice. She saw a woman's restroom and sprinted to it, leapt into a stall, and locked the door.

She knelt before the toilet and, holding her hair back, was sick – and then she was crying. Flushing the toilet, she sat on the floor and sobbed, saying to no one and yet everyone, "Olivia, I'm so sorry. I loved you so much, it's just that I was jealous – and you got to marry that stud Cyril. I have absolutely no idea about whether you were lesbian but camping in Maine sure doesn't say anything about sex. You would have made a poster woman for lesbians: accomplished, beautiful, and witty – oh, so witty – I rather hope you *were* lesbian."

Something dammed up in her burst because of these unusually extreme emotions; but Virginia simply could not stop crying, on the floor of a public bathroom stall. She felt humiliated by the experience, yet powerless to control it. When finally, she tried to stand up, she thought all at once of her assistant Kieran and their amusing conversations – amusing at least to Virginia. Such a nice young man he was, she had handpicked him from that year's crop. My God, she thought, how terrible a way to die. She wondered whether the engine had sucked him through headfirst or feet first.

She began sobbing all over again – in fact she continued to sob for another ten minutes, then she stood up, consulted her phone, all of her employee's contacts were kept handy, and put through a call to his mother out in Sioux City. After an exhausting call, during which she nearly burst out sobbing again, she straightened her dress, unlocked, and left the stall. Her interviewer stood at the sinks, looking at her in the mirror.

Virginia felt as if she were going to faint.

"I'm so sorry," Katie said. "It must be such a challenging time."

'Oh, fuck me blind," Virginia thought, only now recognizing the voice and name, 'I've just been fucking interviewed by Katie Couric.'

"Would you and Buchanan care to join us for dinner? Next week perhaps?"

"But of course," Virginia said, while pretending that it was normal to be washing vomit from your mouth and ignoring the fact that a famed reporter had just overheard a chunk of your life story. "And

I shall see that you are invited to the wedding – no cameras allowed," she said with a smile.

Katie laughed. "I'd be honored."

Alex finished his last lap at the public pool in Fontenay-le-Comte and pulled himself up to the deck. He spied Laurent; sound asleep on one of the loungers. Alex crossed the deck and rolled on top of him, crushed him, smothered him with his mouth. Water dripped down into Laurent's hair, onto his lounger, and Alex took his hands and held them prisoner, Laurent's arms outstretched. Alex kissed him.

"Laurent, I love you."

"I know you do."

"And you? You?" He brought his tongue down the side of Laurent's neck, resting his lips in the soft pocket at the joint of neck and chest.

"*Me*?" He had his puzzled again at English expression, so Alex switched to French.

"You love me too?"

"But of course, I do," Laurent said sleepily, "You are the man I shall love forever." And he gestured as their twin daughters came running through the doors to them, "As do Amelie and Suzette. Oh – it's reminded me. Lizzie and Didier are coming down from Poitiers tonight to stay. It is Lizzie's fertile time and she has particularly requested the room that I hate to clean. However – "

"We're not going to rear another – "

Laurent shushed him and Alex kissed him again. "She and Didier are on their own from here on out. I do love you."

"Us too, Papa Laurent, us too. We love you too."

"Oh," Alex said to Laurent. "I heard from *Monsieur le Maire* today in one of his last official acts. They've decided to stop looking for bones and ash and simply bulldoze everything, cover it with a hill of soil and plant trees there – all the way to our property line, so it will be nice and green and lovely for many kilometers by the time these two are teenagers."

Laurent sucked in his lip and tears dribbled down his face. "What was the last number? Of those presumed to be there?"

Alex signaled to Laurent to try and hold his emotions in check. "About five or six thousand. There's no way to know. But it will be a national monument, built with E.U. money, of course."

Laurent nodded, as if to suggest that was the E.U.'s only purpose. Ruffling the hair of the children, he asked. "Who wants an ice cream?"

They danced in delight.

Mark is the award-wining novelist of *Keeping Gloria Swanson*
and an award winning short story writer,
A proud Québécois, he is presently studying clinical psychology.